D0269022

The Big Freeze

"The earth is already growing cold. The frost will spread, and the snow will fall, and the glaciers will wake and come grinding down from the deep north again, and soon the whole world will be one big snowball, spinning round a cold sun."

"You mean there's going to be an ice age?" asked Buster. He had done ice ages in school, but he'd never imagined them starting in Smogley. "Wicked! Will there be mammoths?"

"You really are thick," sighed the dryad. "I mean, even by human standards. I've known mushrooms with better brains than yours."

Look out for more books in this series:

Night of the Living Veg
Day of the Hamster

PHILIP REEVE

The Big Freeze

**Illustrated by
Graham Philpot**

SCHOLASTIC

Scholastic Children's Books,
Commonwealth House, 1-19 New Oxford Street,
London, WC1A 1NU, UK
a division of Scholastic Ltd
London ~ New York ~ Toronto ~ Sydney ~ Auckland
Mexico City ~ New Delhi ~ Hong Kong ~ Smogley

First published by Scholastic Ltd, 2002

Copyright © Philip Reeve, 2002
Cover and inside illustrations copyright © Graham Philpot, 2002
Mr Bayliss's hair by his mum.

ISBN 0 439 99376 8

All rights reserved

Typeset by Falcon Oast Graphic Art Ltd.
Printed and bound by Cox and Wyman Ltd, Reading, Berks

10 9 8 7 6 5 4 3 2 1

No children's TV presenters were harmed during the making of this book, but
we'll try to do better next time.

The rights of Philip Reeve and Graham Philpot to be identified as the author and
illustrator of this work respectively have been asserted by them in accordance with
the Copyright, Designs and Patents Act, 1988.

This book is sold subject to the condition that it shall not, by way of trade or
otherwise, be lent, resold, hired out, or otherwise circulated without the
publisher's prior consent in any form of binding or cover other than that in
which it is published and without a similar condition, including this condition,
being imposed upon the subsequent purchaser.
So there.

1
HANGING AROUND THE MOUND

"So we're halfway through the first day of our dig here in Smogley," shouted Quentin Quigley, "and so far we still have ABSOLUTELY NO IDEA what this ancient mound here on the playing field at Crisp Street School actually *is*!"

He jumped across one of the little trenches where the archaeologists were hard at work and hurried excitedly around the base of the mound, while a cameraman ran ahead of him to make sure the camera stayed trained on his grinning face.

"Is it the remains of a medieval rubbish tip?" he asked. "Is it a bit of a Norman castle? Or is it really much, much older, as local legends say? Well, so far we haven't unearthed a single find

1

from any of our trenches. But one person who might be able to give us some clues is local lollipop lady, Erica Bayliss!"

"Mum!" hissed Buster. "That's you!"

Buster's mum straightened her spectacles and looked nervous as Quentin Quigley came bounding towards her with his cameraman and sound-person scrambling behind him. The TV people had told her to wear her school crossing warden's uniform, and she looked awkward and out of place in her shiny coat and little black hat, clutching her "STOP" sign.

"Now, Ms Bayliss," said Quentin Quigley, dazzling her with a gleaming white grin. "You're not just an ordinary lollipop lady, are you?"

"Er. . ." said Buster's mum uncertainly.

"In fact," said Quentin Quigley, turning to the camera again, "Ms Bayliss is a keen member of the local history society, and she's the person who wrote to *Dig This!* and asked us to come and excavate this mound. But why?"

Good question! thought Buster. It was embarrassing enough having a history-mad mum who wrote to telly programmes and asked them to dig up mounds, but why had she had to pick on this particular mound? It was just a *mound*, steep and cone-shaped and covered in grass, sitting among the weeds and litter at the far end of his school playing field. It was quite good for rolling down during the lunch hour and getting grass stains all over your shirt, but Buster couldn't see why Britain's third most popular TV archaeology programme thought it would be worth digging up. It wasn't as if it were a castle or something.

"Well," his mum was saying, smiling nervously at the camera. "Well, I've been doing a lot of research on this mound down at the local museum, and I'm sure there's something unusual about it. For instance, did you know that the Bishop of Smogley, writing in the fifteenth century, said there was once a standing stone on the top of it? And on a map of 1642—"

"Stop!" bellowed Quentin Quigley suddenly. "Cut! Hold it!"

The cameraman lowered his camera, the sound-person swung her big furry microphone away and Carla, the programme's producer, came stumbling down the side of the mound to see what the problem was.

"Fifteenth-century bishops?" wailed Quentin Quigley. "Local museums? Come on, Ms Bayliss! We aren't doing some dry old documentary here, you know! This is *Dig This!* We take history and

make it cool and kicking and something the kids will be interested in – and kids aren't interested in dusty old local museums and fifteenth-century bishops! You've got to give us something that will make them sit up and pay attention, Ms Bayliss!"

Buster knew what would make *him* pay attention. He tugged at Quentin Quigley's trendy combat trousers. "'Scuse me," he said, "but what about if you got some blokes and dressed them up like knights and Vikings and stuff and they had a big fight?"

Quentin Quigley blinked at him.

"Buster!" hissed his mum.

"And you need some skeletons," Buster went on. "I mean, if there aren't any skeletons inside the mound to start with, maybe you could borrow one from somewhere else and pretend you found it here." Buster liked skeletons.

Quentin Quigley snapped his fingers at the producer. "Carla, give this kid a *Dig This!* pencil case and get him out of here." He turned back to Buster's mum. "Now, what was all that stuff you told us in your letter, about ghosts and witches and things?"

Mrs Bayliss looked uneasy. "Oh, that," she said. "Well, it's just a lot of silly stories really. Local folklore. Over the centuries, people have always thought of the mound as a haunted place. The local name for it used to be Hob's Hill, and Hob is a traditional name for an evil spirit. . ."

"That's more like it!" whooped Quentin Quigley. "That's what the kids want! Something a little bit spooky."

"We certainly need *something* to spice this show up," muttered Carla as she thrust a pencil case into Buster's hand and pushed him away from the mound. "If the archaeologists don't find something soon we'll have to give up and cancel the whole programme. . ."

Buster watched from behind the barriers with the other spectators as Quentin Quigley went bounding back to his starting position and went all through his opening speech again. This time Mum told him all about the old legends and the hill's name, and he made scaredy faces at the camera and said, "So, join us after the commercial break to see if we find the first *Dig This!* ghost! Whooooooohh!"

Buster sighed. He had thought it would be exciting, having the *Dig This!* team digging up bits of his own school playing field, but it was dull, dull, DULL. On telly, Quentin Quigley came across as funny and clever, but in real life he was just an idiot, always leaping about shouting and flashing his perfect teeth and trying to make out that everybody was having a really good time. (And he was shorter in real life, too.)

The rest of the crowd who had turned up to watch at nine o'clock all seemed to feel the same way, and now the last of them were drifting away, leaving only Buster's brainy Fake Cousin Polly, who was still watching patiently in case something educational happened. Buster's friends the Quirke Brothers had long ago grown tired of waiting to see if the archaeologists dug up a skeleton. Even making faces at the camera had stopped being funny after an hour or so, so they had wandered off. "There's only five more weeks of the summer holidays left, Buster," Harvey had explained. "There must be better things to do with it than this. Come on, let's go down the swimming pool. . ."

Buster would have really liked to go swimming, but he felt he had to stay, out of loyalty to Mum. It had been her idea to bring the *Dig This!* team to Smogley, after all. "I'll try and come along later, maybe," he said, watching wistfully as his friends clambered on to their mountain bikes and pedalled away.

When she had finished saying her bit to the camera Mum came and found him and they both went over to the cluster of TV trucks where Ian, the programme's head archaeologist, was deep in conversation with Carla.

"That's all very well, Ian," Buster heard the producer say as he drew near, "but this is TV, and if your diggers don't come up with something soon, nobody will bother watching the show! Our viewers want to see you solve The Riddle of the Mystery Mound! If you don't unearth a spectacular find before the first commercial break they'll turn over and watch *History Hunt* on the other side. That's why I've sent for a mechanical digger. We're going to stop scraping about on the surface and cut the whole mound in half. That's the quickest way of finding out whether it's really a burial site or just an old pile of earth."

She stomped off, muttering words that Buster wasn't supposed to know as her high-heeled shoes sank into the mud. Ian turned to Buster's mum with a helpless shrug. "I'm sorry about this, Mrs Bayliss," he said. "I've tried explaining to them that real archaeology takes time, but all Quentin Quigley cares about is making an exciting TV show. He says archaeology is the new rock 'n' roll. . ."

"It's all right," sighed Mrs Bayliss, looking up at the steep side of the mound rising behind the catering van. "The council is planning to build houses all over these playing fields in the autumn, so the mound will be gone soon, anyway. And I really want to know what's inside it!"

"Me too!" agreed the archaeologist eagerly. "It's certainly very strange. At first glance I'd have said a Bronze Age burial mound – but where's the body? According to our geophysics machines the mound's solid; no sign of a burial chamber at all. Mind you, they don't seem to be working very well. It's almost as if something inside the mound is interfering with them. . ."

Buster was so bored by now that he couldn't stand up properly and had to slump against the side of a truck. He knew all too well that when Mum started talking about history she could go on for days. He was cold too, which was strange, for the sun was beaming down out of a clear blue sky. He tugged at Mum's coat. "Mum? Can I go home? I'm freezing!"

"All right," she said, handing him her spare keys. "But straight home, mind. I'm going to stay a wee bit longer. . ."

* * *

Buster left her to it. He walked down Crisp Street, past the deserted school buildings and out on to Dancers Road, the traffic-clogged main street that ran ruler-straight through the middle of Smogley. It was warm again once he was away from the playing fields, and he was sweating by the time he reached his own house, number 21 Ashtree Close. He took a can of cola from the fridge and held it against his face before he drank it, staring out of the kitchen window at the back garden with its square of brown grass and its single starveling tree.

Then he ran up to his bedroom and switched on his computer game. He was almost as good as Harvey at zapping evil Zurgoids now, and he was determined to get in plenty of practice so he could beat him next time he came round. But the little screen stayed a dead grey colour, even after he had tried changing the batteries and flipping the "on" switch to and fro and banging it against the wall for a bit. He flung it aside in disappointment and waded through the clutter on his bedroom floor to turn on the telly — only to find every channel full of hissing, spluttering snow.

"Aaaargh!" he said.

It was as if something was interfering with all the electrical equipment in the house. He turned off the fizzing television and flung himself down on his bed to think about it. Outside, traffic snarled and honked on Dancers Road. A train whistle shrieked in the sidings on the far side of the gasworks. A strange voice outside his window shouted, "Buster!"

Buster sat up, startled. His window looked out over the back garden, and there was no way in there from the street. There couldn't be anybody there! Had he imagined the voice?

"Buster!" it called again.

He scrambled over to the window and looked out. There was a girl in the garden, standing beside the tree. She was a funny-looking girl, about his own age but tall and skinny and dressed in a strange sort of old-fashioned, floaty dress. She was certainly nobody Buster knew. But when she saw him gawping down at her she beckoned to him frantically.

He ran downstairs and out on to the lawn.

"Who are you?" he demanded. "What are you doing in my garden? How did you get in?"

The girl looked at him as if she was wondering how he managed to get this far through life without switching his brain on. "I live here, stupid!" she said.

2
TREE'S COMPANY

Buster knew that all girls were pretty weird, but this one really was *very* funny-looking when you saw her close-to. Her long scruffy hair was mossy green, and even her skin had a greenish tint to it. As for her eyes, they kept on changing colour, like sunlight flickering through leaves. She reminded him of something, but he couldn't quite remember what it was.

"Who *are* you?" he asked again.

"I'm a dryad, of course," she snapped, as if it were a perfectly normal thing to be.

Buster frowned. "We did them in school," he said, groping about in his memory for what the word meant. "In Greek Myths and Legends. . ." His brain cells, which had all been having a nice long snooze since school finished, woke up and went grumpily to work. They reminded Buster that he had quite enjoyed doing Greek Myths and Legends. There had been loads of monsters and warriors and stuff, but he didn't think any of them had been called dryads. Now they came to think about it, Buster's brain cells seemed to remember that dryads had been a bit boring. In fact, they were worse than boring: they were *girls*.

"Er, so you're a dryad," he said. "That means you're the spirit of a stream or a river or something. . ."

"That's *naiads*, idiot," snapped the girl, irritably. "Nasty drippy things who hang about in ponds all day feeling sorry for themselves and luring shepherd-lads to watery graves. I'm a dryad. A tree spirit."

"Oh well, near enough," muttered Buster's brain cells. "Can we go back to bed now, boss?"

"To be exact," the dryad-girl went on, "I'm the spirit of *this* tree."

So that was what she reminded him of! Buster blinked up at the tree. There was definitely a resemblance. "Our tree?" he said lamely.

"It's not your tree," she told him. "Or, if it is, you don't look after it very well. In the old days people used to worship trees. They'd leave us presents of wine and cakes and stuff."

"Do you eat things like that then?" asked Buster, who was fond of cakes himself.

"No," she said, "but it's the thought that counts. And a bit of water wouldn't go amiss, you know, once in a while. And what about this?" She lifted the hem of her leafy dress and on her leg, just above her knee, he saw his name spelled out in clumsy scars: BUSTER BAYLISS.

"I wrote that!" he said, aghast. He remembered doing it, back last summer, sitting in the shade of the old tree with his penknife. "It took hours!"

"You're telling me!" agreed the dryad bitterly. "I rustled my leaves like anything, but would you stop? Of course not!"

"Sorry. . ." said Buster.

"Humph," said the dryad.

Buster stared at his feet. He was used to being in trouble, but he'd never been told off by a tree before. Then a thought whizzed through the confusion in his brain and popped out of his mouth. "But how come I've never seen you before?"

"I never needed to talk to you before," said the dryad.

"And . . . you do now?" guessed Buster.

She nodded. "I need to warn you. About what your mother is doing. It's got to stop!"

For a moment Buster couldn't think what she meant. He thought it must be something to do with the garden. Mum had been talking about planting some runner beans – was that what the dryad was complaining about?

Then he understood. "You mean the dig! But how do you know about that?"

"I can feel it in the earth, of course," she said, curling her long green toes down into the lawn. "Why are you humans so stupid? Can't you see the danger? Digging away at Hob's Hill like that! If you're not careful you're going to wake up something that would have been better left asleep! Surely you've seen the signs!"

She pointed with a twiggy finger, past the houses at the back of the garden, over the roof of Tesco, towards the school. A patch of cloud had formed in the sky there. Or was it cloud? Buster squinted at it. It was a flat, swirling greyness, and it looked *cold*. He felt the hairs tingle on the back of his neck. He told himself not to be silly. He was Buster Bayliss, the Terror of 2B! The Phantom Catapult-pinger of Crisp Street School! He wasn't frightened of a bit of old cloud!

But he was. Something about it made him shiver.

"What is it?" he asked the dryad. "What's going to happen?"

"I'm not sure," she replied. "But you've got to stop it! Go and tell your mother and her friends to stop their digging, quickly!"

"But they won't listen to me! They're on telly! Last time I made a suggestion they just gave me a pencil case—"

"Quickly!"

She stepped backwards and vanished, merging swiftly into the old tree. Buster shut his eyes and counted to twenty. He was sure this must be a dream. In a moment he was going to wake up, sprawled on his bed, with his football posters staring down at him.

But when he opened his eyes he was still in the garden. The tree rustled its branches at him meaningfully. The patch of grey still hung above the distant roof-tops of the school. It hadn't grown, but it looked even colder.

He pinched himself once or twice just to make absolutely sure. Then he ran and fetched his mountain bike and set off for the playing fields as fast as his pedals could carry him.

3
BICYCLES AND ICICLES

Two hundred and forty-nine seconds later, Buster skidded into Crisp Street, whizzed past the school gates, zoomed up the slip-road that led on to the playing fields – and almost collided with a mechanical digger coming in the opposite direction. The big yellow machine had a satisfied air about it, and when Buster wiggled past it and rode out on to the playing field he could see why.

Half of Hob's Hill had vanished. Archaeologists and TV people were scrambling around on the freshly exposed earth where the digger had been at work, and Buster could see Mum running up to join them.

Above them, the coldness shifted and stirred and swirled.

"Mum!" shouted Buster. He pedalled frantically across the school football pitch and through the cluster of TV trucks parked on the far side. Near the mound the air was suddenly midwinter cold and the grass under his tyres crackled with frost. Fake Cousin Polly looked round in surprise as he dumped his bike on the ground by the railings, annoyed at him for coming and interrupting just when things seemed to be getting interesting at last.

"Buster?" she said. "What's up?"

"We've got to stop them!" Buster panted. "Something's going to happen!"

"I know," said Polly. "It's really fascinating. Your mum's brilliant, Buster. I wish my mummy was interested in history and archaeology and things, but she's only really into gardening. Do you think we could swap?"

"No chance!" said Buster firmly. He had once had to stay with Polly's family for a few days, and it had been horrible; there'd been no telly in his room, no chocolate biscuits, and he had nearly been eaten by a man-eating alien sprout. "Anyway," he told Polly, "I didn't mean something interesting's going to happen. I meant something spooky and dangerous and weird is going to happen. We've got to stop them digging. . . Brrrr, it's *freezing* here!"

Up on what remained of the mound, people were pulling on fleeces and puffa jackets and flapping their arms to keep the cold out. None of them looked up at the whitening sky, or noticed Buster as he came hurtling towards them. They were all staring at the middle of the mound, where Ian was digging furiously with his trowel.

"Well, we've finally found something!" shouted Quentin Quigley, his breath steaming on the chilly air as he grinned into the camera. "And although it's not quite what anyone expected, it's pretty spectacular! It's not a skeleton! It's not a building! It's a. . . What is it, Ian?"

The archaeologist straightened up and brushed some mud off his nose. "Well, Quentin," he said, "it seems to be some sort of sealed iron vessel. It was buried very deep inside the mound, and we're going to have to be *very, very careful* excavating it, because it really is a unique find, not quite like anything I've seen before. . ."

Buster vaulted over the railings. "Mum!" he shouted. "Mum!"

Mrs Bayliss looked round, but she was too interested in what Ian had unearthed to pay much attention to Buster.

"Let's have a look at it then," Quentin Quigley

said, beckoning for the cameraman to follow him as he scrambled over to join Ian.

"Hang on," the cameraman warned. "I've got technical problems again. . ."

"Me too," said the sound-person, wincing at the whine in her headphones.

But Quentin Quigley had already pushed the archaeologist aside and was reaching down to pick up something small and round, something that the dark earth fell from in frozen clots.

"Now *this* is cool!" he said. Then his smug grin faded. "In fact – it's *freezing*!"

"MUM!" Buster shouted, so loudly it hurt.

There was a blue light, like a flash-gun going off – except that it didn't fade, but hung over the mound, casting weird shadows on the faces of the archaeologists. It looked cold, as if it were filtering through ice. Fog swirled around Quentin Quigley, and a thick frost formed around his boots and spread down the slopes of the mound like a white tide, the grass prickling and ticking as it froze. Something dropped out of the sky and landed with a thud at Buster's feet. He looked down and saw a small bird lying there, its feathers crusted with ice.

"MUM!" he shouted.

He knew that it wouldn't be a good idea to let

that spreading whiteness touch him. He stumbled backwards and scrambled over the railings, pulling Polly with him away from the mound. Behind them, the cold crawled over his bike, freezing it to the ground with chains of frost. Up on the mound his mum and the *Dig This!* team stood still as statues. It was snowing up there, and the snow settled on their hair and faces and cameras and clipboards and they didn't even try to brush the flakes away.

Then the spread of the frost-tide slowed and stopped, leaving Buster and Polly standing on the edge of a circle of winter. Fifteen centimetres from their toes the snow was falling thickly, and the slopes of the mound and the fresh earth of the digging were already white with it. "W-w-w-w-what's h-h-happening?" asked Polly. Her teeth were chattering like demented maracas, and frost had covered her spectacles. "B-B-Buster – your m-m-mum!"

Buster started forward, meaning to go and drag Mum out, but the air near the mound burned with coldness and he jumped back, numbed and shivering. In the blue light Mum and the others glittered faintly, like statues of ice.

And then something moved, up there among the swirling snowflakes. It was Quentin Quigley, still carrying the thing he had lifted out of the excavation, which Buster could see now was a sort of metal jar. He walked slowly down the side of the mound, peering into the frozen faces of Mum and the archaeologists. Then his face flicked towards Buster and Polly. His sun-bed tan had drained away, leaving his skin the colour of fresh snow, and his eyes, which had been blue before, had turned as clear and cold as ice.

"Mr Quigley?" called Polly uncertainly, although it was pretty obvious that this wasn't Quentin Quigley any more.

"What's happened?" shouted Buster. "Is my mum all right?"

The white face stretched and twisted, as if it was trying to remember how to talk. A voice that was not quite the familiar, annoying bray of the TV presenter said, "The time is gone when I was known as Quentin Quigley. . ."

Buster and Polly took another step backwards as the thing glided towards them, but it seemed careful to stay inside its circle of snow. Even with his brain cells on holiday Buster could guess what must have happened. "There must have been *something* inside that jar," he hissed at Polly. "Some sort of evil force! When Quentin Quigley picked it up the lid fell off and it came out and took him over."

"Humph!" said Polly. She was a sensible sort of girl, and she didn't approve of evil forces who went around taking control of other people's brains. "Let Buster's mum go," she told the Quigley-thing, "or I'll, I'll, I'll call the police!"

"Your mother is mine now, boy," the thing hissed, staring hard at Buster. "Here she stays, until the sky freezes and the sun turns cold."

"Well, how long is that going to take?" demanded Buster. "I mean, you can't keep her here all day. Who's going to make my tea?"

The thing's laughter sounded like icicles rattling together in a cold wind. It gestured with one white hand at the rooftops and tower blocks that rose beyond the edges of the playing fields. "What is this?" it demanded. "It was not here when last I saw this place."

"That's Smogley," said Polly.

"It's dirty," sneered the cold thing. "Noisy. Smelly. I will bury it in snow."

"You can't do that!" Buster said. "It's the summer holidays!" But the zone of cold around the mound was already surging outwards. He yelled as he felt the ice beginning to form on his skin, and shook himself free of it and turned to run before he was turned into a frozen statue like the others. Polly ran with him. Snow was falling all around them and the freezing ground was slithery underfoot. Behind them they heard the cold voice shout, "Come back!"

They kept running, past the ice-encrusted trucks and out across the football pitch, sprinting towards the school. As they passed the goal-mouth the ice in the big puddles there suddenly splintered and cracked, exploding upwards in glittery shards like bits of broken window. The pieces collided in mid-air and froze together, forming themselves into two strange, sharp-angled figures, man-shaped ice-sculptures twice as tall as Buster.

Their flat faces swung towards the running children, and their eyes were shifting stains of darkness in the ice. Buster and Polly veered past them, and they gave chase, running with crab-like movements of their icicle legs, reaching out cold hands to clutch at the children as they half ran, half rolled down the slope at the end of the playing field. "This way!" panted Buster, changing course and pounding towards the gates of the school. They were locked for the holidays, but they weren't very high, and he scrambled over them quite easily.

"Buster!" wailed Polly. "We're not supposed to! What if someone sees us?" But she could hear icy claws scraping across the pavement behind her, so she closed her eyes and grabbed Buster's hand and let him help her over. They dashed across the playground, past the music room and the big silver wheelie-bins. The air was warmer here and it hadn't started snowing yet, but the ice things were still behind them, skittering and scrabbling over the tarmac.

"Oi!" bellowed a hoarse old voice. A door slammed open just ahead of Buster and Mr Creaber, the school caretaker, hurried out, brandishing a mop. "Oi! You kids! Hop it!"

"Mr Creaber! HELP!" howled Buster, flinging himself past the astonished old man and turning in time to see the pursuing ice-creatures skid to a halt, uncertain what to make of the newcomer.

"Blimey!" muttered Mr Creaber when he saw them. Then he scowled. "Is this your idea of a practical joke, Buster Bayliss?"

The ice-creatures tilted their heads from side to side, considering him. Then one of them took a few steps forward. It was the larger of the two, and Buster noticed that an old crisp-packet was embedded in the frozen puddle of its face. It reached out sharp fingers and prodded Mr Creaber's chest, and ice crackled over him, binding his feet to the ground, turning his shout of surprise to a puff of steam that hung above his head for a moment and then faded like a failed speech-bubble.

Behind the glassy mask of ice his eyes blinked slowly in sleepy bewilderment.

"Oh, *no!*" wailed Polly.

"Oh, *knickers!*" gulped Buster. He had never imagined that *anybody* would have the nerve to stand up to Mr Creaber. He gulped down a great mouthful of frosty air and they ran on, out of the shadow of the clouds above the school and into the sudden, startling warmth of summer sunshine. The ice-creatures followed them for a little way and then clattered to a stop. Their flat faces glistened with melt-water, and muddy puddles spread around their feet. They waved angry claws at their prey and edged away, back into the shadows and the cold.

Gasping for breath, shivery with running, Buster heaved himself over the school's side gate and hauled Polly after him. Together they stumbled out on to Dancers Road. The traffic was still grinding towards the town centre, shoppers were still lugging their bulging carrier bags out of the supermarket and into spluttering buses and the summer sun was still shining down. Nobody seemed to have noticed the grey, wintry sky beyond the school, heavy with the threat of snow.

"We've got to warn people!" Polly gasped.

"What about your mum and dad?"

Polly shook her head. "Daddy's at work. And Mummy's gone shopping in Bunchester."

"Again?"

"That's just what Daddy said. I think we should call the police. . ."

There was a phone box on the corner by the Indian takeaway, and Buster ran to it and dialled 999 with trembly fingers. But when he put the phone to his ear there was no dialling tone, only a soft, sighing hiss, like the wind over snow-drifts. "They probably won't believe us anyway," he said bitterly. "They'd probably remember me from that time me and my friend Tundi rang up and said there were a load of vampires hanging round the churchyard. They'd think it was another joke. And even if they believed me I don't see how they could help. Something extra-weird is going on. So we need somebody extra-weird to help us stop it. . ."

"But who?" asked Polly, looking worried. She couldn't imagine anybody much weirder than Buster.

"I know just the person," he said. "Well, she's

not a proper person, she's a tree, but she'll know what to do. Come on. . ."

"*A tree?*" said Polly incredulously, but Buster had already slammed out of the phone box and set off again at a breathless run, and there was nothing for Polly to do but shrug and follow him.

4
TALKING TO TREES

It looked as if there was a party going on in Buster's back garden. He had been hoping that the dryad would be waiting for him there, but when he burst out of the back door he saw that there was now a whole crowd of girls gathered around the old tree, twittering and whispering together with a noise like rustling branches in a storm-tossed wood.

"Who are they?" cried Polly.

"Dryads," said Buster.

"Dryads? But there's no such thing as—"

"At least, I suppose they are. There was only one before. Maybe this lot are the spirits of Mum's geraniums or something."

Polly looked critically at the girls, their spindly

bodies and their silvery, stripy skin. "They don't look like geraniums. I think maybe they come from the birch trees on that little traffic island at the end of your road. Listen to that way they keep coughing and sneezing. It must be because of the car fumes. . ."

"Well," said the first dryad, the green girl, pushing her way through the twittery crowd and coming up to Buster. "You made a proper mess of that, didn't you?"

"It wasn't my fault!" Buster protested angrily, but he was glad to see her. After the cold Quigley-thing and the ice-monsters there was something nice and ordinary about talking to a tree. "There was this *thing* inside the mound," he told her, "and Mr Quigley opened it and now he's gone all strange and Mum and the rest are frozen solid like fish fingers and there were these ice-things that chased me. . ."

"And Mr Quigley isn't Mr Quigley any more," Polly put in. "He's turned into something different, something all *cold*. . ."

The birch-tree dryads clustered together, whispering, shaking their rustly heads. "He's awake!" they hissed. "He's come back! Oh! Oh! Oh!"

"What?" asked Polly. "What do you mean? Who's awake?"

The birch-people just whispered and quivered until Buster felt like shaking them, but the green girl said, "Something old. Something very old and very powerful, from the time before the first seeds sprouted and the first forests grew."

"From the stone time," the others whimpered, shivering. "From the ice time!"

"He was bound with iron and magic," she went on, "and held inside the hill, and now your mother and her friends have let him out."

"Stop being mystical!" shouted Polly. "Who are you talking about?"

"He is the Winter King," the dryad said. "And his power will grow and grow now he is free. I can feel it in my roots. The earth is already growing cold. The frost will spread, and the snow will fall, and the glaciers will wake and come grinding down from the deep north again, and soon the whole world will be one big snowball, spinning round a cold sun."

"The land covered in snow!" quavered the other dryads. "The waters bound in ice! We'll die! We'll die!"

"You mean there's going to be an ice age?" asked Buster. He had done ice ages in school, but he'd never imagined them starting in Smogley. "Wicked! Will there be mammoths?"

"You really are thick," sighed the dryad. "I mean, even by human standards. I've known mushrooms with better brains than yours."

"Yes," agreed Polly. "Don't you see, Buster? What she's talking about would mean. . . It would mean the end of the world!"

"Ice age, stone age," the birch-dryads whispered. "Nothing mortal can live where the Winter King rules."

"Then it's up to us, Buster," Polly said. "We're the only ones who know about this, and we'll never get grown-ups to believe us – well, not in time, anyway. It's up to us to save the world!"

"Oh, not *again*," said Buster. "We're *always* having to save the world, and it's the school holidays, too. Why can't somebody else have a go for a change?"

"We've got to stop him!" Polly insisted. "We sorted out those alien sprouts last term; we can sort out this Winter King too. We'll stop him, and make him unfreeze your mum!"

Buster didn't want anything more to do with the Winter King. He wanted to run back inside and slam the door and eat beans on toast and watch TV and wait for Mum to come home and tell him that everything was all right. But Mum would not be coming, and he could see the patch of winter that hung above the school, looking bigger now and colder, as if the sky were dying.

"What do you mean, stop him?" asked the green girl. "There is nothing a mortal can do to stop the Winter King. Soon his icelings will be everywhere, freezing everything that lives. He is full of the old magic. Only wizards can fight that."

"Wizards?" said Buster. "You mean, like, magicians?" He was thinking of Mr Hinksey at number 23, who ran a joke shop and sometimes did conjuring tricks at the school Christmas party.

"No, a *wizard*," snapped the dryad. "It was wizards who bound the Winter King and trapped him in the hill, and if it wasn't for you stupid humans there would be wizards still who could put him back there. But the wizards are gone, or sleeping."

"Gone where?" demanded Polly. "Sleeping where?"

"Are they on the phone?" added Buster. "Would they be in the Yellow Pages? Can't we wake one up?"

The dryad shrugged like a tree in a gale. "Nobody knows where they are, not any more. Who can read the lines of the land through a crust of concrete? How can the old power flow when you lot keep filling the earth up with sewers and and pipes and tunnels and TV cables? Humans! You're almost as bad as the Winter King!"

"No, we're not!" cried Polly. "We like trees! I do, anyway. I recycle newspapers and everything!"

"Newspapers!" wailed the birch-tree dryads, shuddering in horror.

Buster looked pleadingly into their pinched, silvery faces. "All right," he said. "We'll show you! We're going to find one of these wizard blokes, and make the Winter King stop."

The dryads whispered, whispered, talking tree-languages that he couldn't understand.

"But we need to know where to start looking," he went on. "You'll have to tell us."

"How would I know?" asked the green girl sulkily. "I'm just a tree. I can't help you. You had a chance to stop the Winter King waking, and you fluffed it. Now there's nothing to be done but go inside our trees and wait for the end; wait for the ground to freeze and the sun to go out and the ice to shatter our boughs."

"Nothing, nothing, nothing to be done!" the others whispered. They were starting to fade, turning into silvery wisps of air that flickered up and away over the roofs of Ashtree Close, home to their thin stand of trees on the traffic island. Soon only the green girl was left.

"Pleeeease," said Buster.

"Oh, all right," she sighed. "Ask the fair folk. They won't be hard to find. All sorts of old things will be stirring now. They'll feel the fabric of your world starting to fray, and they'll come back from the places where they've been hiding. The fair folk might tell you where a wizard sleeps, if you can get any sense out of them at all. . ."

"Brilliant!" said Buster, then remembered that the world was ending, Mum was frozen stiff and he was talking to a tree. "Well, brilliantish."

5
SWINGS AND ROUNDABOUTS

The dryad faded back into her tree, leaving Buster and Polly looking bewildered in the empty garden. "Fair folk?" Buster said. "Who on earth does she mean?" The only fair folk he could think of were the ones who parked their roundabouts and rifle-ranges on the wasteground by the canal for a week each summer; they were big and burly and covered in tattoos, and shouted at you if you stood up on the waltzers, but he didn't think they were very magical.

"It sounds a bit familiar," said Polly, frowning. "I know, your mum's into history, isn't she? I bet she's got a dictionary of myths and folk tales. I'll look it up. . ."

She went into Buster's mum's study to search

through the bookcase, and Buster hurried upstairs to his bedroom and started scrabbling through the heaps of stuff on the floor. Eventually he found his rucksack, and into it went his gloves, his hat, his Smogley United scarf and a spare jumper. Running back downstairs, he hunted through the kitchen cupboards until he found some biscuits, then made some hot chocolate which he poured into Mum's thermos flask. (It was a bit of an embarrassing thermos flask, because Mum had got it cheap in the sales and it was for kids really, with brightly coloured cartoon characters dancing all over the outside of it. But if everybody was busy being frozen, they probably wouldn't notice.) He dug his warm winter parka out of the back of the hall cupboard, and found Mum's old duffel coat which he thought would more or less fit Polly if she rolled the sleeves up. Finally he went to Mum's room and found the catapult that she had confiscated last month after he smashed one of the panes of glass in Mr Hinksey's greenhouse.

Polly was waiting for him by the front door. She pulled the duffel coat on and they went out together into the front garden.

"I looked up 'Fair Folk'," Polly said.

"Brilliant! What did it say?"

"Promise you won't laugh?"

"Of course."

"It's an old name for fairies," said Polly.

"Fairies?!!!" Buster didn't exactly laugh, but he went a funny purpley colour and made a noise like a coffee machine having a bit of a turn. "But there's no such thing as fairies!"

Just then something whooshed past his head and thunked into the wood of the front door. He turned to stare. A small white arrow with pale green feathers stuck quivering just above the letter box.

"Buster!" shouted Polly. "Look!"

Over on the traffic island, figures darted and scampered between the birch-trunks. They had a flickery, not-quite-there look, but Buster glimpsed broad green faces and beady eyes and heard peals of high, thin laughter. Another arrow clattered on the pavement at his feet, and then the fairies were zipping away down the close, bouncing on the roofs of parked cars and firing their bows at the big topiary rabbit in Mr Hinksey's front garden.

"Bloomin' hippies!" bellowed Mr Hinksey, running out of the house in his washing-up apron and shaking his fist in the direction of the fading laughter. "Firing arrows about! You'll have

41

somebody's eye out!" He saw Buster and Polly watching him and hurried over. "Are you all right, kids? That's the third bunch of oddballs I've seen this afternoon, all heading towards the park. Weird-looking lot. Is there a pop festival or something going on? It's the first I've heard. . ."

Buster and Polly left him glaring at his pin-cushioned shrubs as they hurried on down the road. "The park!" said Polly. "If we hurry we can catch up with them there. . ."

"But they shot at us!" Buster objected, not sure he really wanted to catch them up. "With arrows!"

"I think they were just trying to scare us," Polly explained. "Your mum's book said that fairies are supposed to be mischievous. Tricksy. They like making trouble."

"So do I," said Buster, "but I don't go firing arrows at people. At least, only ones with suction-cups on the end. . ."

But Polly wasn't listening; she was trotting off towards the park, and Buster couldn't help noticing that she could move surprisingly fast for someone so round. He scurried after her through the quiet streets of the estate, following the fairies' trail of dented cars and kicked-over wheelie-bins.

* * *

The park should have been busy on this sunny school-holiday afternoon, but by the time Buster and Polly hurried in through the north gate a chill wind had begun to blow and all the mothers and children and dog-walkers were heading for home. "Hasn't it turned nippy?" Buster heard one woman say as she passed, and her friend said, "You can't trust the weather forecast. . ."

"Look!" Polly pointed towards the children's playground at the bottom end of the park. Green figures were running riot between the swings, twirling on the roundabout and whizzing down the slides. Polly and Buster ran towards them, passing a couple of sniffling children whom the fairies had kicked off the climbing frame. As they drew nearer they could see that the fairies were cobwebby creatures, their spindly bodies almost transparent and constantly changing shape so that it was hard to tell exactly what they looked like. Sometimes they seemed to have wings and sometimes they didn't, but they seemed just as happy in the air as on the ground. They flitted around Buster's head like bats as he opened the gate into the playground, and one forced Polly's mouth open and reached inside, shouting, "Give us yer gnashers! Give us yer gnashers!"

"Tooth fairy," guessed Buster, batting it away.

"Silly humans! Fatso! Scruff!" A mothy shape came whirling down off the top of the plank-swing and flickered in front of them. "What do you want?" it asked. "Get back to your mumsies! Go to bed and pull up the covers! Make hot-water botties! Winter's coming, didn't you know? No place left for silly humans, soon!"

It flung itself away with a wild laugh, bounced off the rubbery surface under the swings and shot up into the sky. Another took its place, leering into Buster's face. "You can't stop the Winter King! The cold's coming back and we don't care. Earth and water, snow and ice, it's all the same to us. Put a stop to horrid humans, though! You'll freeeeeze, and we're glad, glad, glad!"

"You don't mean that!" shouted Polly, brushing fairy hands out of her hair. "We need your help. We need a wizard to stop the Winter King. . ."

"And you'd have one, too, if it wasn't for humans," said a fairy, landing on top of her head. It perched cross-legged there and picked its nose, flicking the bogeys at Buster. "Who ever heard of a prison without a guard?" it asked. "When the

wizards locked the Winter King up they left a guardian, a sleeper to guard a sleeper. But the Winter King's awake now, and the guardian's still snoring. His alarm clock hasn't gone off, dozy old wiz!"

"Where can we find him?" asked Buster. "Is he inside Hob's Hill too?"

"Don't you know *anything*?" the fairies sneered. Buster felt small hands tying knots in his hair and fumbling about in his rucksack. Fairy bodies surrounded him, flickering like old home movies, flashing rainbow colours where the sun shone through them. "Look between the Dancers," they urged him teasingly. "The Hill and the Dancers and the old straight path between, that's how it should be, that's how it would be, *if* it weren't for silly humans. . ."

They rushed away, a flash of pale shapes like dirty plastic bags blowing between the trees, a peal of laughter echoing. The door of the park-keeper's hut banged open and Mr Curd came huffling out, pulling on his cap. "What's going on?" he shouted when he saw Buster and Polly. "Where'd they go?"

Buster shrugged. Mr Curd looked round the empty playground, then pulled off his cap and scratched his bald, pink head. "I could have sworn

I saw somebody. . . Somebody mucking about on my swings. . ." But the swings dangled empty, and the roundabout was slowing to a standstill.

Polly leaned close to Buster and said, "We've got to go."

"Go where?" he asked. "They were no help at all. They didn't tell us anything. . ."

"I know, but we've got to go away from here," said Polly.

Something soft and feathery brushed against Buster's face. He reached up to shoo it away, but it wasn't a fairy. Another touched him, and another.

"Funny weather we're having for the time of year," muttered Mr Curd.

Buster looked up. The sky above the park was wintry grey, and already the first big flakes of snow were falling.

6
IN AT THE DEEP END

Buster and Polly hurried past the ornamental bandstand towards the exit on the far side of the park. The snow wasn't laying yet, but the air was growing colder by the minute and it could not be long now before the boating lake froze and the fountains stopped playing and the park became part of the Winter King's white domain. Buster munched miserably on a biscuit and wondered why the world had to end right in the middle of the holidays. Why did this sort of thing never happen in term-time, when at least there'd be the consolation that you were missing school?

"'A sleeper for a sleeper,'" said Polly, frowning to herself as she tried to puzzle it out. "That's what the fairies said. 'The Hill and the Dancers and the old straight path between.'"

"I know what they said, but what's it mean?" Buster grumbled. He was feeling fed up. He had thought the fairies were going to help them, not lark about and talk a lot of rubbish and go giggling off into the trees.

"The Hill must be Hob's Hill, where the Winter King was bound," Polly mused. "So the Dancers must be somewhere nearby. Another hill? Have you heard of anywhere around here called the Dancers?"

Buster shook his head. "Only Dancers Road. I can't imagine a wizard sleeping there, there's too much traffic." But his mind was starting to work. "I wonder why it's called Dancers Road, though?" he said. "It's a funny sort of name, isn't it? Maybe its named after something that was there before the road was built."

"A place where people danced?" suggested Polly.

"Like a disco or a dance-hall. . ." suggested Buster.

"I wouldn't have thought you'd get much sleep there either, even if you were a wizard," Polly said.

"I think we should ask the Quirke Brothers,"

Buster decided. "They know loads more about this sort of thing than I do. They're bound to know all about wizards and things, because they play those sword and sorcery computer games, and they read big fat books called things like *The Rune-Sword of Spib* and *Elf-Kings of Nimby*, specially Cole."

"Well," said Polly doubtfully, "I don't know if that really qualifies them to. . ." But she had no better ideas. She glanced nervously over her shoulder at the boating lake, wondering how many of the Winter King's icelings would soon be hatching from its freezing waters. "All right then. Do you know where to find them?"

"Easy-peasy," said Buster. "They're at the pool."

* * *

The swimming pool at the Leisure Centre was huge, built not long before as part of Smogley's failed bid to host the Olympics. It had diving boards and wave machines and a giant anaconda slide, and there were so many children splashing around in its chloriney waters that Buster and Polly had trouble spotting either of the Quirke Brothers among the crowds – especially since they still had their shoes on and weren't allowed on the pool-side. They made their way along the front row of the benches where the mums and dads and teachers usually sat to watch the school swimming gala. "Harvey! Cole!" they shouted, but with so many other excited voices echoing from the high roof there wasn't much chance of any Quirke Brothers actually hearing them.

At last they spotted Harvey. At least, they noticed a sort of pink lightning-bolt shooting into the pool nearby and the lifeguard blowing his whistle and shouting, "Oi! Can't you read? No Cannonballs!", and when the lightning bolt climbed out it turned out to be Harvey.

"Where's Cole?" yelled Buster.

"Diving boards!" Harvey shouted back, zooming off to have a go on the anaconda slide.

Cole was standing on the lowest diving board, trying to summon up the courage for a dive. "Cole!" yelled Buster, hurrying towards him, and he looked round and waved, then came and sat on the diving-board steps, glad of an excuse for not plummeting into the choppy water. Buster couldn't help noticing that he had rather natty swimming trunks with starfish on.

"You stay here," he told Polly, not really wanting the Quirke Brothers to know that he was going around with Polly again. He left her perching on the benches and hurried towards the diving boards, going as close to Cole as he could get without letting his forbidden trainers touch the tiles at the edge of the pool.

"Hullo!" said Cole, pushing his wet hair away from his face. "What's up? Fancy dress?"

"Eh?"

"Well, you look like you're pretending to be an arctic explorer or something. And I can't work out what Polly's trying to look like at all. . ."

"Oh," said Buster with a shrug. "You know, fake cousins. She just sort of happened to follow me in. And it's turned a bit cold outside, actually. That's what I wanted to see you about. You know all about wizards and stuff, don't you?"

"Well, I'm up to level 42 of *Dungeon of Doom*," agreed Cole, looking rather pleased with himself.

"Do you know where they sleep? It's just, I've, er. . ." Buster's brain whirred and creaked, trying to work out how best to explain things to his friend. It was going to take ages, and he didn't have ages. He settled on a Brilliant Plan. "It's just that I've been playing this computer game, and there's this wizard I've got to wake up, and he's supposed to be sleeping at somewhere called the Dancers, but I don't know what it is. Any ideas?"

Cole looked thoughtful. "Probably a stone

circle," he said wisely. "They're pretty wizardy places. In the old days there were often legends about them, that they were dancers who had been turned to stone, and they came to life and danced on Midsummer's Eve and stuff. So the Dancers would be a pretty obvious name for one. Is there a stone circle in this game of yours?"

"Errrr," said Buster, trying to think if he had ever heard of a stone circle in Smogley. His gran was part of a knitting circle, but he didn't think that was the same thing at all.

"Oh, look," said Cole. "Somebody else in fancy dress. He looks even sillier than you. . ."

Buster glanced towards the pool entrance, and let out a yelp of terror. Striding in through the suddenly ice-bound turnstiles was Quentin Quigley, dressed now in shimmering robes of ice and with a tall crown of icicles upon his head and a single huge icicle held like a staff in one hand. Behind him, almost invisible in the shadows, came a flickering, spidery army of scuttling icelings.

"It's the, it's the, it's the. . .!" spluttered Buster, pointing.

"It's the what?" asked Cole.

Then everything started happening at once. The lifeguard went running over to where the Winter King stood and the shrill peal of his whistle was cut off short as the Winter King's staff prodded him on his chest-wig and turned him to ice. The icelings came clustering forward, still unnoticed by most of the people playing in the pool. Buster ran to Cole and started pushing him towards the entrance, but Cole slipped on the wet tiles and went plunging into the pool. At the same moment, down at the shallow end, the Winter King touched the lapping waters with his staff, and the whole pool became a single enormous chlorine-and-wee-flavoured ice cube. The splash that Cole had made froze into a strange white sculpture, and when Buster looked down he could see his friend trapped inside the ice like a fish in a frozen pond.

"Cole?" he shouted.

"Buster! Don't just stand there! Run!" Polly cannoned into him from behind, pushing him off the pool-side down on to the ice as a gang of icelings came scuttling towards him. He slipped over, scrambled up, slipped again, and Polly pulled him up and dragged him after her across the frozen pool, while people came stumbling half-dressed from the changing rooms to see why it had suddenly gone so nice and quiet, and the Winter King and his minions went quickly from one to the next and froze them into surprised-looking statues.

Buster and Polly slithered across the pool like very bad ice-dancers, the icelings in hot pursuit*. In the silence, a single voice rang out, coming from somewhere above: a muffled, spiralling, "Wheeeeeeeeee!"

"This way!" yelped Buster, realizing what it was, and shoving Polly towards the mouth of the anaconda slide. As they passed it the voice from inside grew louder: "Wheeeeeeeeeee!" it went. They could hear the sound of a be-swimming-trunked bottom rushing towards them down the spiralling plastic tube, and got out of the way just in time. The icelings on their tail were not so lucky; they were right in front of the slide when Harvey shot out of it, crashing into them and smashing their icy bodies into scattering bits. "Wheeee. . . Ooh!" he said, startled at landing on ice instead of water, and went skittering off towards the far side of the pool, where the Winter King was waiting with his staff.

"Harvey! Watch out!" wailed Buster, but it was too late; by the time the words were out Harvey was a popsicle, and already more icelings were starting across the frozen pool towards Polly and Buster.

"Come on!" Polly shouted, and he let her haul him up an icicle-draped ladder on to the

*Oh, all right then, cold pursuit.

pool-side and out through a side entrance into the street.

They ran and ran until the air grew warm around them and they realized that they were outside the Winter King's spreading zone of cold – at least for a while.

"He saw us!" whispered Polly. "He must know we're up to something. He'll be hunting us now. . ."

"Hurp, hurp, hurp, hurp, hurp, hurp," said Buster, who was a bit out of breath.

"Anyway," Polly went on, "did Cole tell you anything interesting before he got frozen?"

"Hurp, hurp, hurp," said Buster.

"And please stop going 'hurp'."

"Hurp, hurp, sorry, hurp, hurp," panted Buster, and scoffed a biscuit to restore his strength while he thought back over what Cole had told him. "He said the Dancers was probably a stone circle, but I've never heard of a stone circle in Smogley. . ."

"I expect it's been knocked down to build a car park or something," said Polly wisely. She knew that Smogley Town Council couldn't look at an ancient monument or a beauty spot without thinking how much nicer it would be with a car park on top of it.

A little light bulb appeared above Buster's head – at least, it should have, because he had just had a brilliant idea.

"I've just had a brilliant idea!" he said. "I bet you're right! What if there was a stone circle right here in Smogley once, and all that's left of it now is the name of Dancers Road? Dancers Road is straight, like the straight path those stupid fairies were going on about, and if the Winter King's mound was at one end, the stone circle must have been at the other. . ."

He dived back into his rucksack and pulled out the street-plan. There was Dancers Road, running straight from school to the far end of town.

"And your mum said there used to be a standing stone on Hob's Hill, too," Polly muttered, running her finger along the road on the map. "I bet it used to line up with the circle, and Dancers Road follows the line of the old path between them. . ."

"Then that's where we'll find the guardian, if we are going to find him at all," Buster agreed. He studied the map. It was a long way, and the Winter King's grip on Smogley was tightening fast; already the air around them was growing cold. "There's a bus stop outside Woolworths!" he remembered. "Come on!"

It was still summer in this part of town, and Buster and his fake cousin were hot and sweaty inside their winter clothes by the time they reached the bus stop. The grannies and young mums aboard the bus all stared at them as they found a seat, and Buster heard them whispering, "Ooh! Look! Loonies!" But after a couple of stops the sunshine faded and the air inside the bus turned chill, and soon the other passengers were all looking enviously at Polly's duffel coat and Buster's nice warm parka. Buster and Polly ignored them. They knelt on the back seat, staring through the grimy window at the grey, dead patch of sky which hung over Smogley town centre like the belly of an invading UFO, and at the thick flurries of snow which were starting to whirl up Dancers Road.

Polly's tummy made grumbly noises. "Did you bring anything to eat except biscuits?" she asked hopefully.

"Er . . . no," Buster admitted.

"What, no fruit or sandwiches or anything?" She rummaged about in Buster's rucksack and came up with biscuits, biscuits and more biscuits. "Honestly, Buster, don't you know that too many biscuits are bad for you? Haven't you ever heard of a balanced diet?"

Buster thought that biscuits and more biscuits was a very well-balanced diet, but he didn't say so, because he knew that Polly was one of those people who believe in healthy eating and no snacks between meals and other strange stuff. "I could lick the chocolate off for you," he suggested helpfully.

"Oh, *Buster!*" said Polly, deciding she wasn't hungry after all.

Half an hour later they reached their stop, and stepped out on to the litter-strewn pavement under the motorway flyover at the unfashionable end of Dancers Road. "Thank you!" Polly said politely to the driver. The bus roared off, driving round a loop of road with a boarded-up pub in the middle and heading back towards the town centre.

Buster looked around for signs of stone circles or anything else a bit magical-looking. There wasn't much to see. Apart from the old pub standing abandoned in its weed-grown car park there was only a bingo hall and a discount carpet warehouse, and the metal roofs of the industrial estate poking up from behind a wall. The concrete pillars of the flyover were scribbled with graffiti and the roar of the traffic overhead boomed out across the empty lots. Buster had never seen anywhere less magical in his life.

"Well," said Polly. "Where's this stone circle then?"

Buster tried not to let her see how disappointed he was. "I didn't say it *was* here," he reminded her. "I said this is where it *used* to be." But even if there *had* once been a stone circle at the end of Dancers Road, he couldn't see where it had stood. A cold wind from the town centre stabbed through his thick parka like icy needles. He pulled the collar up tight around his neck and wondered what to do next.

"Come on," said Polly. "Let's look around. . ."

She took a step forward, and would have slipped head-over-heels if Buster had not reached out to steady her. While they stood talking a film of black ice had formed on the pavement. Snow started to fall, spilling down on them as if a giant chef was sifting flour through a ginormous sieve somewhere high above them. Around them the sky was still clear, but above their heads a long tentacle of cloud had uncurled, blackboard-dark, stretching the whole length of Dancers Road.

"He knows we're here!" gasped Buster.

"He knows *something's* here!" said Polly. "You were right, Buster! There's something around here that he's afraid of! If only we could see it. . ."

A sudden crackling noise made them both spin round. Icelings were lifting out of the ruts and puddles in the empty lot. They were man-high, bristling with dead leaves and sweet wrappers, and their flat faces were the shape of arrow heads.

Buster unslung his rucksack and found his catapult, then squatted down and felt around on the pavement until he found a good missile – a rusty old hinge from a broken door. His mum had strictly forbidden him to play with the catapult any more after the Mr Hinksey's Greenhouse Incident, but he didn't think she would mind him using it now, considering how the future of all life on earth was at stake and everything.

The icelings were edging towards him slowly, twitching their icy heads from side to side as they tried to work out what he was doing.

"What *are* you doing?" asked Polly.

Buster fitted the hinge into the catapult sling and pulled it back as far as it would go, taking careful aim at the nearest iceling. Then, *spannnng, CRASH!* The iceling folded and burst in a spray of glittery fragments, and crumbs and shards of ice went skittering away across the tarmac. The others made creaky noises and drew back in dismay.

"Quick!" shouted Buster.

They ran together across the loop of road where the bus had turned and into the car park of the old pub. The ground underfoot was covered with gravel and odd piles of rubbish that people had dumped there over the years. Buster snatched up a good-sized stone and turned in time to smash an iceling that was reaching out for Polly. She crouched beside him and scrabbled for fresh ammunition.

Then it was pitched battle, with Buster pinging his catapult as fast as he could reload while Polly heaped up piles of pebbles and old bolts and sometimes hurled half a brick or a clod of crumbled tarmac at any icelings who came too close. The creatures swarmed and scuttled towards them in spiky waves, and burst with a sound like a hundred greenhouses being kicked over a cliff. Twice their ice-shard claws nearly touched Buster, but each time he broke them at the last instant and they dropped away from him like shattered mirrors.

And then, quite suddenly, the dark clouds overhead reared back and lunged down towards the pub like a cold snake striking, except that instead of poison they spat hailstones. Hailstones the size of marbles came hissing around Polly and Buster, hailstones the size of golf-balls, hailstones the size of hens' eggs, hailstones the size of grapefruit that burst into a thousand stinging fragments when they hit the ground. Buster raised his arms to shield his face, and the hailstones punched and pummelled at him, hurting even through his thick winter clothes.

"Well, this is fun!" shouted Polly, but Buster thought she was probably being sarcastic.

The storm swung over the car park like a bead curtain. Behind it the icelings watched and waited, and behind *them* a tall, shimmering figure came gliding down Dancers Road, the Winter King in his robes of ice, come to join the fun.

Polly ran to try the boarded doors and windows of the old pub, but they were nailed shut and she could see no way to prise them open. There was nowhere to shelter from the battering downpour. Then, as she stooped for a brick to fling at the waiting icelings, she noticed the old pub-sign lying forgotten in a clump of nettles. She heaved it up and dragged it to where Buster crouched, holding it over them both like a shield. The

drumming of the hail on the thick wood was deafening, but it protected them from the worst of the bombardment and they were able to scratch about for more bits of stone, ready for the icelings' next attempt.

Suddenly, as if the Winter King realized that he had been outwitted, the storm ceased. Polly cautiously lowered the sign. That was when Buster noticed the name on it – the name of the old pub. In peeling letters on the hail-pocked wood were the words, *The Nine Dancers*. There was a not-very-good painting underneath of nine girls dancing round a green knoll crowned with standing stones.

He was so excited that he couldn't speak for a moment. He tugged at Polly's arm and gurgled.

"If you're having an idea, you'd better have it quickly," she said. "Look!"

Out on the road the drifts of hailstones were melting and running together and refreezing to form shards and spines and twitching iceling bodies.

"It's here!" said Buster, showing her the sign. "This circle of land with the pub on it! This is where the stones used to stand!" He looked at the pub. It was an old building and its walls were made of the same brown stone as a lot of the houses and shops in Smogley, but down at the corner of the front door he noticed a stone that was bigger and darker than the rest, and another next to it, laid on its side. He was sure they must be parts of the old circle. They had been dragged here from the mountains of Wales and set up to mark the place where the guardian lay sleeping, ready to wake if the Winter King stirred under Hob's Hill. But people had forgotten what the old stones meant, and over the years they had fallen down and been carted off to make walls and houses. Then, when the pub was built, the last two stones had been used in the front wall!

Crackling, creaking noises came from the road. Some of the new icelings were swarming up the flyover supports on to the motorway. There was some angry hooting, then the sound of the traffic thinned and stopped as they went from car to car, locking them under ice. The rest, led by the Winter King himself, came creeping towards the pub, patient as a glacier.

Buster ran and pressed his hands against the old stones, but they were just stones. He wasn't sure what he had expected. He beat his hands against their rough old flanks and shouted "Help! Help!", but no wizard rose from beneath the crumbled tarmac to put the Winter King to flight.

In the snowy silence he could hear the icelings creaking closer. "Buster!" shouted Polly again, as if she thought he might not have noticed the danger.

Overhead the black clouds swirled, and the numb, cold wind howled between the flyover supports. "Foolish children!" hissed the Winter King. "Stop meddling! Come here and let me freeze you!"

There has to be something here, thought Buster. *Otherwise why would he be going to all this trouble to stop us?*

He looked at the stones again, and saw the prints of his hands outlined there in silver. At first he thought that it was a trick of the frost and the winter light, but they grew brighter and tracks of silver spread across the two old stones like veins in a leaf, wrapping them in a pale glow. Light bloomed in the crack where the two stones met, spilling across the car park like the glow from an opening door.

The icelings hissed and hid their faces as well as they could behind their see-through claws.

"Stop!" bellowed the Winter King.

An opening had appeared between the two stones, although when you looked hard you could see that they hadn't really moved. A tall, thin shape stood silhouetted against the wash of silvery light.

"Who dares disturb the slumber of –" it began, and then said, "Oh, crikey heck! Icelings? Already?"

"Help!" wailed Buster, scrambling towards the light.

"All right, all right, keep your hair on," the silhouette grumbled. "Don't get your Y-fronts in a flurry. Come in, if you're coming. And I suppose you'd better bring your friend, too."

"Stop them!" howled the Winter King, and his icelings surged forward in a last, desperate rush, spilling towards the front of the pub like a cold wave. Their claws reached out for Polly, but Buster grabbed her by the duffel-coat toggles and pulled her after him through the gap between the stones. Then the portal vanished, and the charging icelings slammed into the solid wall of *The Nine Dancers* with a noise like a herd of frisky bulls having a knees-up in the world's biggest china shop.

7
SLEEPING BEARDY

Buster was confused at first. He knew that the doorway he had just stepped through wasn't a *real* doorway, but somehow he had still expected it to lead to the inside of the derelict pub. Now, looking around, he didn't feel quite so sure. He had never actually been inside a pub before, but he definitely hadn't expected so many stalactites. *Maybe it's one of those theme-pubs you hear people talking about,* he thought.

In the strange silvery glow from the rocky walls he could finally see the person who had rescued him. It was a tall, thin man, wearing a brown robe that seemed to be made of the same material as Mr Creaber's school caretaker's coat, but which had even more pockets and hung all the way down to the floor. His wrinkled face was half-hidden by an enormous, bushy beard, and he wore a leather cap with a candle stuck on the top. Dribbles and splatters of wax had run down over his face and plopped on to his shoulders, and feathery little wax stalactites hung from the old stubs of pencils which he had stuck behind his ears.

"Are you a wizard?" asked Polly.

"Do I look like a bloomin' wizard?" asked the man, sticking his beard out. "I'm a dwarf, I am."

Buster and Polly both squinted up at him. "You don't look like a dwarf, either," Buster said.

"What d'yer mean?"

"Well, shouldn't you be a bit shorter?" Buster asked.

The dwarf looked offended. "Me dad was a dwarf," he said. "Me mum worked for the Gas Board, though. I suppose I do take after her a bit, in the height department. But I'm a dwarf all right. The name's Len. Hundreds of years my family's been looking after this place. We serve the guardian, you see. Keep his white steed ready and his staff and spell-books nicely dusted ready for him to wake up and do battle with the Winter King if he ever gets out of Hob's Hill."

"But he *has* got out of Hob's Hill!" cried Buster. "He's turning the whole of Smogley into one big freezer-cabinet, and he's frozen my mum and there's icelings everywhere!"

"Don't I know it!" grumbled Len. "Hundreds of years we've been keeping ready for this, and now the time's come and the guardian won't wake up. I blame you humans. Dug up the old straight path, didn't yer? Pulled down the stones. Mucked up the mystic alignments. Now look at the mess we're in! Icelings! Already! It'll be trolls and ettins before the night's out, you mark my words."

He turned and hurried away, stooping under low-hanging stalactites. Buster and Polly ran after him. "Who is this guardian?" Polly asked, and her voice echoed and echoed from the vaulted roof. "Can we see him? Maybe we can help wake him. . ."

"Huh," snorted Len. "You can try if you like." He didn't sound hopeful. "Oi!" he suddenly bellowed. "You goblins! Hop it!" There was a stifled burst of sniggering overhead and Buster looked up in time to see some small grey shapes scurrying away, swinging like monkeys from stalactite to stalactite.

After a little way the rocky passage widened

and the low roof rose, and Buster realized that they were in an enormous cavern, where pillars and stalagmites of multi-coloured stone rose out of a dark and silent lake. "I never knew there were any caverns under Smogley," he said, hoping to get on Len's good side. "They're brilliant!"

Len looked pleased. "Dwarfs hollowed this lot out," he said, leading the way to a place where a bridge of living rock spanned the dark waters. "Lovely bit of work. Look at them stalactites. You don't see craftsmanship like that these days."

"I should have thought there'd be guided tours and potholers and stuff," Buster went on.

"Potholers?" The lanky dwarf shuddered with disgust. "If you think I'm going to let a bunch of scruffy herberts with torches stuck to their heads go prannying about in my caverns, you've got another think coming. No human knows of these places, except for you. Anyway, the only way in is by magic, through *The Nine Dancers*. Now come on, hurry up."

* * *

Afterwards, Buster was never sure how far the dwarf caretaker led them through the maze of caverns. He had vague memories of spiralling corridors, and of galleries where the stalactites and stalagmites clustered so thick that it was like wandering through a a forest of stone trees. He remembered crystal pools where blind white fish drifted, and caverns where the echoes of his footsteps rang out like the school orchestra's xylophones, only in tune. But when they finally reached the centre of it all and Len ushered them into the cave where the guardian lay sleeping, it somehow felt as though they hadn't come very far at all.

"There he is," grumbled Len.

The wizard sat in a chair of silver-veined stone at the centre of the cavern. He looked like an old, old man, tall and bony, his skin like pale parchment, his eyelids grey, as if the colour of his eyes was showing through the thin skin. His bony hands were folded around a long staff that lay across his knees, and his white beard trailed over them and down on to the floor between his pointed shoes. You would have thought he was dead, except that he was snoring loudly and from time to time his nose twitched.

"He should have woke up as soon as all this nonsense started," explained Len. "That was what

the Brotherhood of Wizards had in mind when they stuck him down here all those years ago. He was meant to wake up at the first sign of trouble and mount his white steed and go riding off to put the Winter King back in his Hill. Only he's overslept. Well, they can't blame me. I've done my job. His white steed's all ready and everything."

He nodded to an alcove in the rock-face behind the wizard's chair, where an old Triumph motorcycle stood, handlebars gleaming in the dim silver light.

"That's not a steed!" complained Polly, who had been hoping to see a nice pony. "It's not even white! It's a sort of creamy colour, with silver bits!"

"It's the best I could do, under the circumstances," sniffed the dwarf. "Have you ever tried keeping a horse in a cave for thousands of years? The mucking out's a nightmare. And you have to exercise it somewhere and find it some grass to scoff, and where could I do that in Smogley these days?"

Polly frowned. "Couldn't you just have made the horse go to sleep, like the wizard?" she asked.

"Course I couldn't!" snapped Len. "Don't you

bloomin' humans know anything? Only a wizard can sleep that long and still hope to wake up again. Put a horse or a human or any other dumb animal into a magical sleep for more than a week or so and that'd be the end of them; their spirit would get bored and potter off somewhere else. That's what'll happen to the folks the Winter King's frozen, if we don't thaw 'em out sharpish."

"Like Mum, you mean?" cried Buster, horrified. "But we can't let her spirit potter off! She's still using it!"

"Ah, but the Winter King doesn't care about that," said Len gloomily. "He just wants their bodies, you see. He hasn't got a body of his own, so he steals other people's."

"Yes," nodded Buster. "He's inside Mr Quigley at the moment; we saw him. . ."

"And when that body's used up he'll hop into your mum's or one of the others," explained Len. "He's just keeping them on ice until he needs them. Pity we can't wake old sleepy-head here up and do something about it."

"We've *got* to do something!" said Buster. He wasn't ready to admit defeat, whatever Len thought. He ran to where the wizard sat and shouted "WAKEY WAKEY!" into his hairy old ear hole. He shook him, but it was like trying to shake a rock. He tried pulling the old man's beard, then tweaking his nose. He bent down and pulled his pointy shoes off and tickled his feet. The wizard twitched a bit at that and mumbled, "Eh? Whassat? Shut the door, Mr Cauliflower-head! Pardon, Mother? Booble. . ." Then he was fast asleep again, snoring even more loudly than before.

"See?" said Len, gloomy but satisfied. "Useless! It's all you humans' fault. There used to be an avenue of standing stones that ran from Hob's Hill to the Dancers, see? The old straight path, we called it. If it was still there the ripples of the Winter King's awakening would have come flooding through and roused the guardian. But your lot took 'em down, didn't you? Built a bloomin' road over them. Crossroads and roundybouts and traffic lights and discount carpet warehouses. Plays havoc with your mystical alignments, all that sort of thing."

Buster gave a sigh of annoyance and kicked a stalagmite. Grown-ups were rubbish, he decided, even magical ones who lived in enchanted caverns. Then he hopped about a bit clutching his toes and reminding himself not to kick any more stalagmites because it really really hurt. "Oh, all

77

right," he said when he had finished. "We'll do it ourselves."

"Eh?" said Len.

"Well, it can't be that difficult, can it?" Buster insisted. He picked up the wizard's staff and twirled it. It was made of wood, and it felt heavy and ordinary, more like a broomstick than something magical. "This'll defeat old icicle-features, will it?" he asked.

"No!" yelped Len. "I mean, yes, but only in the hands of a wizard! I mean. . . Put that down, you cheeky little—"

"Buster's right," said Polly firmly. "If your wizard can't be woken, someone else is going to have to do his job. What do we have to do? Do we just point the staff at him? Are there any magic words?"

"But, but, but. . ." gibbered Len. Then he looked thoughtful and started pacing up and down, studying the walls of the cavern. "Well, I suppose there's a chance. Especially if the Winter King's got your mother, boy. If there's blood involved. I suppose you might be able to rouse the old magic before he freezes you. . . As for words, I don't know. I'm not a wizard. I suppose you could say a few words of power if you want. Don't know what they'd be, though. . ." He shook his head. "No, no, it wouldn't work. Too risky. Besides, what if old beardy-weirdy here wakes up and needs his staff? I'd look a proper charlie, wouldn't I, telling him I gave it to some nippers. . ."

He looked round, waiting for Buster and Polly to agree with him. But while he had been muttering to himself, they had slipped quietly away, taking the staff with them.

"Oi!" shouted Len. "Oi! You kids! Get back here with that!"

His shouts echoed after the children as they scarpered up long stairways and through a cave where ancient hands had painted beautiful pictures of mammoths and bison and dancing stick-men on the walls (although the cave-goblins had scribbled moustaches and silly hats on most of them).

They had planned to go back the way they came, hoping that the icelings would not still be waiting for them outside the boarded-up pub. But the caverns had changed somehow: there were passages and stairs that they didn't remember, and the ones they did seemed to have twizzled around and be leading in different directions. "Oi!" came Len's voice, echoing between the stalagmites behind them. "Oi! You little blighters!"

"This is useless!" panted Polly. "We should have left a trail of string, or breadcrumbs. . ."

"We haven't got any string or breadcrumbs," Buster pointed out. He was starting to think that they would never escape from these caves. His trainers slithered and skidded on the damp floors, the staff kept tripping him up and he had already banged his head on at least five stalactites.

Then, quite suddenly, they came to a narrow cleft in the rocky wall. A familiar smell came from it, something like a cross between Buster's sock drawer and a school dinner.

"Eugh!" they both said.

But better a bad pong than an angry caretaker. They squeezed through the crack, and found themselves in a very unmagical-looking tunnel built from crumbly red brick, where a walkway led along the side of a sluggish stream.

"Smogley main sewer, I think," said Polly, holding her nose.

"Lovely," agreed Buster.

A ladder of rusty iron rungs led up through a shaft in the roof of the sewer. At the top was an ordinary manhole cover. Buster, encumbered by the awkward staff, couldn't make it move at all, but after a bit of grunting and straining and some fairly naughty words* Polly managed to heave it open.

Morning light poured in on them, and with it came thick, white flurries of snow.

8
THE FROZEN WORLD

Buster blinked in surprise as he scrambled up out of the manhole, realizing that something had gone wrong with time while they'd been in the caverns. It seemed only a few minutes since he had dragged Polly through the front wall of *The Nine Dancers*, and it had been early evening then. Now it was the middle of the following day. "Time must move faster inside the caves," he said, "the same way it moves slower in geography lessons. . ."

The Winter King had been busy overnight. Snow covered Smogley like a billion-tog duvet, and more was falling steadily. The whisper of the falling flakes was the only sound that Buster could hear. He wondered if the whole world was like this now, but through a gap in the fog he glimpsed green summer hills beyond the edge of town. So far, winter had come only to Smogley.

"I hope Mummy and Daddy are all right," said Polly. "They probably couldn't get home last night. Mummy will be furious if the frost's got at her petunias. . ."

Buster was starting to work out where they were. This was one of the new housing estates at the top of the hill on the far side of the Smogley to Bunchester canal. One of the boys in his class lived near here, and Buster and his friend Ben had come to watch videos at his house in the Christmas holidays. He looked around to see if he could recognize it, but the houses had looked pretty much alike to start with, and now they were identical, with snowdrifts heaped up against the doors and bars of ice on all the windows. On either side of all the streets were rows of sad little white hummocks that Buster realized must be parked cars.

There was nobody about, no distant grumble of traffic from the city centre, nothing but the falling snow and the pale sun glittering on the drifts.

"At least I can't see any icelings," he said, pulling up his parka hood.

"I suppose they've done their work," agreed Polly. "They're probably back at Hob's Hill putting their feet up, or playing ice-spy, or whatever else the forces of evil do on their days off."

"Well, that's where we've got to go," said Buster. "That's where Mum is, remember?" He looked down at the wizard's staff in his hand. In daylight it looked even more like an old broom handle than before, and he suddenly didn't feel quite sure that he was going to be any good at defeating the Winter King's magic. Polly watched critically as he held it up in the air and posed with it. "Do I look like a wizard?" he asked.

"Not really," she admitted. "You look like a great big twit."

"I thought so," said Buster miserably. "Maybe I could find someone else who could use it. Mr Hinksey can do magic. Do you remember how he pulled all those handkerchiefs out of his hat?"

"I'm not sure that was actually magic," said Polly.

"Of course it was. There were loads of them. And he was going to saw one of the dinner ladies in half, but she chickened out. I bet *he* could use this to fight the Winter King."

But as they set off towards home along the deserted streets, Buster began to suspect that Mr Hinksey was probably frozen solid by now, along with everyone else in Smogley. They passed ladies with prams and shopping bags, a man talking into his mobile phone, some children with a football, but all of them had been frozen into ice-sculptures. Icicles dangled like bunting from overhead cables. In one place a car had skidded and hit a lamppost as its driver froze. Its engine had caught fire, but even the flames had frozen, encased in ice like bits of orange coral inside a paperweight. The placard outside a newsagent's shop carried the headlines of yesterday's *Smogley Evening News*: FREAK BLIZZARDS SMOTHER SMOGLEY! WEATHERMEN BAFFLED!

It was tiring, ploughing through all that snow. The cold scorched Buster's face and stung his eyes and burned in the back of his throat, and his breath came out in thick grey puffs until he started to feel like a steam engine. After about ten minutes he found that his fingers and toes had gone numb, and after another ten it seemed as if he had been walking for ever. Once they heard the distant clatter of rotor-blades and glimpsed a helicopter buzzing between the tower blocks in the town centre, but it soon stopped, and afterwards the town seemed even quieter. And once they had to hide while two huge, hairy creatures lumbered past, breaking chunks off of people's garden walls and eating them.

"Flippin' Ada!" hissed Buster, cowering behind a snow-bound car. "What are they? Abominabubble Snowmen?"

"Trolls, I think," Polly whispered back, remembering her quick trawl through Mrs Bayliss's book of folklore. "It's like your dryad friend said: all sorts of magical creatures are stirring now that the humans are out of the way."

The trolls tramped off to gnaw at the concrete of the multi-storey car park in Pooley Street, and Buster stood up wearily, ready to start trudging onwards. But Polly stayed crouching in their hiding place. She sniffed the air. "Green!" she said suddenly.

"What is?"

"I can smell green!"

"How can you *smell* green? That's like saying you can hear orange."

"I just can!" she said. "I mean, a sunshiney, gardeny sort of smell, like in Mummy's greenhouse."

Buster had a quick sniff. He couldn't smell anything, but Polly's mum was a maniac gardener,

and Polly was pretty keen on plants and stuff herself, so if she said she could smell a garden he supposed she must be able to smell a garden. How it had managed to avoid being frozen, however, he couldn't begin to guess.

"It's this way!" said Polly eagerly. "Come on!"

She hurried off. Buster ploughed after her, through drifts of powder snow, muttering rude words that turned into twisty grey clouds as soon as they got out of his mouth. By the time he caught up with her again she was turning on to Steeperton Hill, a posh street that led down towards the shops on the canal-side. It was lined with big, semi-detached houses, all cold and silent now under their cosies of snow.

All except one.

Halfway down the street stood a house that the snow had not touched at all. Its front garden was an explosion of brilliant colour, with roses and hollyhocks and lupins all jostling for space. In the black-and-white world that Smogley had become it stuck out like a flamingo trying to gatecrash a penguin's birthday party.

"Told you so!" said Polly, and ran to peer over the front gate. "Isn't it lovely! I hadn't realized how much I'd been missing flowers and grass and things. . ."

Buster joined her, gaping at the sunlit house as if it were a mirage which might disappear at any moment.

Instead, the front door opened and a little white-haired old lady came pottering out, wearing a sun-hat and a flowery dress and carrying a watering can. When she saw Polly and Buster staring at her she pulled the hat off and waved it at them.

"Hello, dears!" she called. "My, don't you look chilly! Why not come inside for a nice cup of tea?"

9
THE PERILS OF FAIRY CAKES

"I'm Mrs Marjoriebanks, my dears," the old lady explained, showing them through into her sunny living room. "And these are my friends Miss Pugh and Mrs Parker-Hartley."

Two more old ladies perched on the edge of the sofa, clutching plates of cake and cups of tea. They both looked rather like Mrs Marjoriebanks, round and pink and cheerful, but Miss Pugh's hair was blue and Mrs Parker-Hartley's purple. Behind them a big French window opened on to a back garden just as lush and flowery as the front. Buster couldn't help noticing that the falling snowflakes simply disappeared about five metres above the lawn.

"I don't understand!" he said. "How come you haven't been frozen like everybody else?"

"Aha!" exclaimed Mrs Marjoriebanks. "I wondered when you'd notice that! What a clever boy you are!"

"The thing is," said Miss Pugh, "we are all members of the WI, so we have the power to resist the Winter King and his little games."

"What does she mean?" asked Buster, nudging his fake cousin.

"The WI," Polly explained. "It's short for 'Women's Institute'. Mummy's a member, too."

"I know what it *means*," said Buster. "I just didn't know they had special powers. Not unless making lemon curd is a special power. . ."

"No, dears," explained Mrs Parker-Hartley sweetly, "not the Women's Institute. The *Witches'* Institute. We're witches."

"People are always getting us mixed up," admitted Mrs Marjoriebanks. "I suppose the names are rather similar. . ."

Buster opened his mouth to say, "But there's no such thing as witches," then thought better of it. After all, until recently he had thought there were no such things as dryads, fairies, trolls, dwarfs, goblins, icelings or Winter Kings. Witches weren't really such a big surprise. In fact, he wouldn't have been very surprised if the old ladies had turned out to be the Loch Ness

Monster, the Easter Bunny and the Beast from 20,000 Fathoms. "You are. . . I mean. . . You are *white* witches, aren't you?" he asked them nervously.

"Oh yes, dear, yes, of course," they all said quickly, nodding. "Ever so white!"

"Then you must take this!" said Polly happily, grabbing the wizard's staff from Buster and handing it to Mrs Marjoriebanks. She breathed a sigh of relief, glad to have found some nice, sensible grown-ups to take charge of things. "You must have the power to stop the Winter King and make everything normal again!"

"Ooh, what a lovely broom handle!" the old lady trilled.

"Looks old," nodded Miss Pugh.

"Antique, I'm sure," agreed Mrs Parker-Hartley admiringly.

"But it's not for us, dear," Mrs Marjoriebanks concluded, passing it back to Buster. "This is wizard magic, you see, and we are witches. We wouldn't have the power to *fight* the Winter King. Only to keep our little house nice and safe and snug."

"But. . ." said Polly desperately.

"Now, dears, you must be hungry," she went on, steering Buster to a comfy armchair. "I'm sure you'd like some tea, and a nice cake?"

"And maybe the little girl would like a stroll around our garden?" Miss Pugh chimed in. "You look as though you're a plant-lover, dear!"

Polly nodded happily. Buster wanted to tell her to wait, because he wasn't quite used to the idea of these kindly, unfreezable witches and didn't want to be left alone with them, but she was already following Miss Pugh out into the back garden, and Mrs Marjoriebanks was already pressing a plate into his hand. It was full of fairy cakes with thick, pink icing and frilly paper wrappers and hundreds-and-thousands. He put down the wizard's staff so that he could eat one, and Mrs Parker-Hartley balanced a cup of tea on the arm of his chair.

The cake was just about the nicest thing he had ever tasted. He wolfed it down and started on another. He had forgotten how hungry he was. But he still hoped he could persuade the witches to help him. "*You* know all about the Winter King," he reasoned. "There must be something I can do that would stop him."

The old ladies watched him eat and nodded, smiling.

"I mean, I broke the icelings with my catapult. Would a catapult work on him?"

They shook their heads.

"Then what if I could find a really big hair-dryer? Or a gun or something?"

"Oh, no, no, no," they said. "No, a gun would never do. No mortal weapon could harm the Winter King. You would only kill the poor mortal body he has stolen, and he would find another to go into."

"The Winter King is not a *person*, you see," said Mrs Marjoriebanks. "He is more like a form of energy. Perhaps he started as a cold spark, given off by a glacier grinding over stone. . ."

"He's a thought," said Mrs Parker-Hartley, rubbing her bare arms as if just talking about it was giving her goosebumps. "He's the *idea* of winter. You can't hurt an idea, can you?"

"And he's getting stronger all the time," explained Mrs Marjoriebanks. "So far, he's only frozen Smogley, but his magic waxes with the moon. When the full moon rises tonight he will be at his most powerful, and by tomorrow morning the whole world will be his."

"So you're really much better off just staying safe and snug with us," said Mrs Parker-Hartley.

"Safe and snug," her friend echoed.

"But my *mum*. . ."

"Now, I expect you're sleepy," said Mrs

Marjoriebanks. "You do *look* sleepy, dear. Sleepy, sleepy, sleepy."

Buster hadn't really thought about it until she mentioned it. Now he realized that he had been up all night. Suddenly he was yawning. His eyes felt gritty, and he could not keep them open. "But what about Mum?" he murmured. His head was nodding, and the throws and cushions piled in the armchair seemed wonderfully soft.

"That's it, dear," said Mrs Marjoriebanks brightly. "You lie back and have a nice little snooze!"

"But Mum. . ." he whispered, and then he was asleep.

The snow fell soft and quietly through his dreams. It piled up all round him and covered him over until he felt as if he was inside a big, crisp meringue. He was partial to a nice meringue, so he'd have been perfectly happy there if it had not been for an annoying little voice that kept shouting, "Buster! Buster! BUSTER!"

He opened his eyes.

He was not in a comfy armchair any more.

He was lying face-down on a floral patterned tablecloth, and his arms and legs were tightly bound.

"BUSTER!" shouted Polly's voice, muffled and

far away, as if she was still out in the garden and all the windows were shut – and when he listened more closely he noticed that she was shouting not "Buster" but "Guster".

He twisted his head round, saw the bottom of a fridge, heard kitchen noises. Feet in fluffy slippers shuffled about, and Miss Pugh's voice said, "It's no good, girls — we're never going to fit him in the microwave."

"Well, he won't go in the oven," said Mrs Parker-Hartley.

"We'll have to chop him up," suggested Mrs Marjoriebanks. "Or what about mincing him?"

"But the spell says he's to be roasted *alive*," insisted Miss Pugh.

Buster gave a great heave and managed to turn himself over so that he was lying on his back. He was on the kitchen table and the three witches were clustered around him. Mrs Marjoriebanks clutched a cleaver, Mrs Parker-Hartley held an electric whisk and Miss Pugh had her glasses on and was peering at a book called *Cooking with Kids*.

"Bother!" said Mrs Marjoriebanks. "He's woken up!"

"I *told* you to put more sleeping potion in the cake-mix, Matilda," sniffed Miss Pugh.

Buster wriggled desperately, but his hands and feet were tightly tied with lots and lots of baby-blue knitting wool. "Let me go!" he shouted. "What are you doing?"

"The thing is, dear," said Mrs Marjoriebanks happily, "we're going to have to roast you."

"Alive!" added Miss Pugh.

"It's all because of that horrible old Winter King," explained Mrs Parker-Hartley. "The local witch-forecast says that all this snow and ice is set to last for a least ten thousand years. If our little nest is to stay sunny and snug and safe from icelings for all that time we're going to have to protect it with some very powerful spells. A human sacrifice usually works best, we find."

"*Roast alive one boy, then sprinkle his juices around the boundaries of the place to be protected,*" said Miss Pugh, reading from her book.

"Of course, we'll eat you when we've finished, so you won't go to waste," promised Mrs Marjoriebanks.

"And if there's any left over," added Miss Pugh. "we'll have you cold, in sandwiches."

"We're so glad you came by, Buster," beamed Mrs Parker-Hartley. "We thought we were going to have to thaw out one of our neighbour's little boys, and it's never the same, cooking from frozen. . ."

Buster looked from one smiley old face to another. He could barely believe what he was hearing. "But you said you were *white* witches!" he reminded them.

"Well, maybe not *white* exactly," tittered Miss Pugh.

"The difference between black and white is not as great as most mortals seem to think, Buster," Mrs Parker-Hartley told him.

"I suppose we must be in the middle somewhere," Mrs Marjoriebanks decided. "You can think of us as sort of creamy-grey, off-white witches, if you find it helps."

"GUSTER!" wailed the voice from the garden.

"What have you done to Polly?" he shouted.

"She's in the garden," said Mrs Marjoriebanks. "We're going to keep her there."

"We've always wanted a lovely statue in our garden," added Mrs Parker-Hartley. "So we've turned her to stone. A little girl is so much prettier than a gnome. Though we'll have to find a way to stop her shouting like that. Nobody likes a shouty statue."

"And she's a bit on the plump side," added Miss

Pugh. "So we might have to chip a bit off her round the edges. . ."

"No!" howled Buster, but Mrs Marjoriebanks stuffed a big ball of wool into his mouth to keep him quiet. "Mmff brbbffllbmlbb!" he spluttered.

"Tut-tut," chided Miss Pugh. "Language!"

"Now, dears," said Mrs Marjoriebanks, turning to her friends. "All this talk of gardens has given me a splendid idea. If we can't roast young Buster in here, why don't we do it outside?"

"A barbecue!" the others cried, and clapped their chubby hands together in delight. "Oh, what fun!"

10
STONE ME!

It had been lovely at first. Polly had pulled her soggy socks and boots off and walked about barefoot on the enchanted lawn, sniffing the flowers and admiring the shrubbery, feeling sure that there would be some way to persuade those nice old witches to help tackle the Winter King.

But when she saw, through the French windows, the witches dragging Buster's helpless body into the kitchen, and tried to run and help him, Miss Pugh had tapped her on the top of the head and muttered some incantations and she had found herself freezing as solid as one of the Winter King's ice-statues. She had looked down and seen her bare feet actually turning into stone. Then Miss Pugh had lifted her head up, saying,

"Chin up, dear; we don't want a statue that's going to stand about staring at its feet for all eternity, do we now?"

And so here she stood, looking like something you'd find in a garden centre and feeling a complete idiot for ever having trusted the three old ladies. But strangely, although she was stone on the outside, she was still Polly on the inside. She could still think, she could still see, and she could still speak, although her mouth was frozen in a round gasp of surprise so it was a bit difficult to make the words come out right.

"Oh, gother!" she said. "Guster! Guster!"

She could hear voices in the kitchen and a clattering of cutlery, and once she thought she heard Buster shout out, "No!" She strained all her muscles, trying desperately to move towards the house, but she was stone.

"GUSTER!"

Then something hit her in the face, cold and sharp and splattery, and she heard high, thin laughter rippling down from the rooftops.

On the roof of the house next door pale figures flickered and spun, chasing each other round the frozen chimney pots and swinging from the drainpipes. Thin fairy hands scooped up more snow and packed it tight and flung it down at her.

"Stupid statue!" jeered the fairies. "Stone me! Ha ha ha!"

"Helb!" Polly begged them. "Please! Helb be!"

"Can't even talk straight! Gottle of geer! Gottle of geer!" A fairy came whirring down and hovered in front of her. Its eyes looked like the markings on a moth's wing. Its smile was a fence of sharp white teeth. "Help how?" it asked.

"Stob the widges!" begged Polly. "Shoob them with your abbows!"

The fairy shrugged, and the others shook their heads and turned out empty pockets. They had just had a brilliant fight with a gang of pixies outside Sainsbury's and all their arrows and bows had been lost, or broken. "No help for you, rock-face!" they sneered. "No help for the scruffy human boy, neither. Why should we help you anyway? Winter's here. All you silly mortals will pop your clogs. It'll be just us then, and we're glad, glad, glad!"

"Oh, please helb," Polly whispered. "We'b gob to geb back to 'Ob's 'Ill and fight the Winder Kig. . ."

The fairy, which had lost interest in Polly and darted off, suddenly fluttered back in front of her again. Its friends crowded closer, whispering to each other in their little insect voices. "What? Fight the Winter King? *You?*"

"Me an' Guster," said Polly, "yeb."

"What, just the two of you?"

"Yeb. We'b gob a bagic staff. . ."

Shrill squeals of laughter burst from the fairies, almost deafening her. They writhed about on the lawn and spun helplessly in mid-air clutching their sides. This was the best thing they'd heard for centuries! The idea of a couple of kids with a stick trying to defeat the mighty Winter King! It was priceless! This they had to see! They shrieked and screamed and howled and wept and wet themselves with laughter, and several of them burst.

"Well?" demanded Polly, mustering as much dignity as it's possible to muster when you've just been petrified in a posture of mild surprise. "Are you goig to helb us, or nob?"

* * *

Miss Pugh took hold of Buster's legs and Mrs Parker-Hartley took his arms and between them they dragged him out into the garden. Mrs Marjoriebanks brought up the rear, wearing a plastic apron with "Chef" written on it and dragging a big bag of barbecue briquettes. Buster kicked and writhed and struggled but the old ladies were a lot stronger than they looked. They hauled him past the place where Polly stood trapped and down to the end of the garden, where there was a little patio and a bench and a brick-built barbecue.

"Come on, Myrtle, come on," shouted Mrs Marjoriebanks, chivvying her friends along. "Come along, Hilda, no slacking. Now, lift him up, that's right, and – Ooogh!" A snowball hit her full in the face, making a loud "chuff" as it burst against her glasses. She stumbled backwards and dropped the bag of briquettes in an ornamental pond.

"Stupid witches! Nyah-ner-de-ner-nerrr!" Moss-grey shapes came whirling past like leaves on an autumn gale, sticking out their long green tongues and pulling horrible faces. More snowballs hurtled down. Some hit Buster, but most hit the witches. There was a flurry of wings in the flower-borders, and clods of earth and uprooted plants went tumbling high into the air.

"My lupins!" bawled Mrs Parker-Hartley. "My lobelias! Ooh, you little *beasts*!"

The fairies veered and flickered, now here, now gone, thumbing their noses and weeing in the birdbath. One flipped Mrs Marjoriebanks's apron over her face. Another shoved handfuls of freezing snow down the back of Miss Pugh's dress.

A couple stood on the roof of the potting shed and flashed their bare green bottoms.

"Horrible little hooligans!" spluttered Mrs Marjoriebanks, tugging the shed door open and vanishing inside. Buster thought she must be trying to seek shelter from the fairies, but a moment later she came scurrying out again, carrying the biggest aerosol can he had ever seen. He glimpsed the label as she hurried by; it said SPRITE-B-GONE, and there was a crossed-out picture of a fairy.

The jeering fairies fled towards the house in a cobwebby cloud and Mrs Marjoriebanks danced across the garden, spraying them with great clouds of elficide. A couple were hit and dropped with faint thuds on to the lawn, where they lay with their tongues sticking out and their legs in the air. The rest clustered into the narrow passage that led down the side of the house to the street. They ripped the heavy side gate off its hinges and threw it out into the road, then whirled around the front garden tugging up rose-bushes and drawing dirty pictures on the lawn. The three witches charged after them, Mrs Marjoriebanks squirting her spray-can, Miss Pugh with a raspberry-cane and Mrs Parker-Hartley waving an uprooted lupin and shouting, "Beasts! Oooh! Little beasts!"

"Guster!" shouted Polly. "Rug for it! Guickly!"

He couldn't really run, bound as he was hand and foot, but he rolled off the barbecue and managed to hop across the lawn to her as if he were in training for the sack-race. "Mf annnt gb wbbrrp goo!" he said.

"Got gid you gay?"

"Mf mfb: 'Mf annnt gp wbbrrp goo!'" Buster spat out the ball of wool and spluttered a bit. He had the feeling that he would be pulling blue fluff out from between his teeth for a very long time. "I can't go without you!" he said again.

"I'b trabbed," she told him. "Bub you can escabe, gile they're gusy wib the gairies. . ."

Buster bunny-hopped over to the side-passage and peered past the splintered posts where the gate had been. The fairies were out in the street now, dancing on snowbound cars and shinning up the lampposts, while the witches stood in the front garden shouting furious spells and squirting puffs of SPRITE-B-GONE. A few dead fairies had crashed into the snowdrifts (Buster could see their legs sticking out), but the rest didn't seem to care. "Can't catch us!" they taunted. "Silly old trouts! Wrinkle-stockings! Pudding-hats! Blue-haired bumblers!"

The infuriated witches opened the garden gate and charged out into the street – which was exactly what the fairies wanted them to do. In front of the house was a place where the snow had been tramped and smoothed by fairy feet until it was as hard and slippery as an ice-rink. One after another the three witches went head-over-heels, and the fairies whirled down to jeer and taunt and tickle, rolling them out into the middle of the street where the snow was thick and soft. "Oh! Agh! Hee hee! Stoppit! Ooohh!" the witches wailed, helpless against a hundred eager little hands. They started to roll, a tangle of arms and legs, gathering speed as the street steepened. The fairies snickered, and darted up on to the rooftops to watch the fun. "Argh!" howled the witches, wrapped in one giant snowball now, with here and there a hand sticking out, or a slippered foot or a bit of a blue-rinsed hair-do. Faster and faster they rolled, until it made Buster feel giddy just watching, and then they reached the distant bottom of the hill and crashed into a deep drift outside the bus station, and thick white snow closed over them.

"Useless old biddies!" jeered the fairies, spiralling up and away like wind-blown litter.

A last snowball splatted on top of Buster's

head. He shook it away. Snow was falling on the witches' house and their green front garden. Overhead the dark sky bellied downwards and spat a fierce blizzard of white flakes, as if the Winter King had suddenly become aware of this unsightly patch of green in his cold, clean world and wanted to cover it quickly.

Buster kicked himself free of the blue wool (which had been loosened by all that bunny-hopping), and went back on to the lawn.

Polly was wriggling her toes. As the witch-magic faded she was slowly turning back into a girl. She could feel the soil beneath her feet again, cooling as the fingers of the frost reached into it. Shivering worms curled against her toes for warmth, then slid away as she tried moving her feet. She was free – but she wasn't about to tell Buster that.

Polly's mum was keen on Positive Thinking, and Polly had often heard her say things like "If you believe you can do something, you can!" and "Self-confidence is all it takes." She didn't altogether believe it – after all, dotty Uncle Alfred sometimes believed he was a chicken, but he'd never managed to lay a single egg. *On the other hand*, she thought, *it just might work*. If she could convince Buster that he could use the wizard's staff to work magic, perhaps that would give him the upper hand when it was time to confront the Winter King. . .

"The staff!" she called, when he came running to her. She made struggly motions to make it look as if she was still at least half statue. "Fetch the wizard's staff!"

Buster blundered back into the house. It was changing fast as the witch-spells unravelled, the flowers on the wallpaper wilting, the scent of pot-pourri changing to a sour stink of cats. The staff was still there, though, solid and dull as ever on the suddenly threadbare sofa. He snatched it up along with his rucksack and ran back to the garden, where Polly waited on the whitening lawn.

"Quickly!" she pleaded.

"But I still don't know what to do!" said Buster. He waved the staff half-heartedly at her and tried to remember the magic words that Mr Hinksey used when he was about to find 50p up someone's nose, or pull a hat out of a rabbit. "Er. . . Abracadabra!" he shouted. "Nicky-Nacky-Noo! Shazam!"

Nothing very obviously magical happened, but Polly lifted first one foot and then the other, stretched her arms, jumped up and down. "Buster!" she said. "You did it!"

"Did I?" Buster looked at the staff again. It hadn't changed at all. "But I didn't do anything!" he protested in a feeble voice.

"Yes, you did!" Polly reached out to touch his hand. "Don't you see? You have power over the staff! The magic comes when you call it. I bet Len knew that all along."

"But. . ."

"Now, quickly," she said, looking terribly serious. "We'd better get back to Hob's Hill and see if you can use your powers against the Winter King."

Buster suddenly remembered what the witches had told him, about how the Winter King's power would be complete once the full moon rose. That didn't leave them long to get right the way across town. . . "We'll never make it!" he started to say, but a Brilliant Idea came whizzing out of his brain at the same moment and headed the words off before they could get to his mouth. "I know!" he said instead. "I've got this brilliant idea. . ."

The heavy wooden gate from the witches' side-alley was still lying in the snow where the fairies had dropped it. Buster dragged it out into the middle of the road. "Quick, climb on behind me and hold tight!" he ordered, scrambling aboard.

"Are you sure this is a good idea, Buster?" asked Polly, but she did as he said, locking her arms round his chest, and he used the wizard's staff to get them moving, pushing it into the snow like a paddle.

The makeshift sledge edged forward and began to gather speed. Soon it was rushing down Steeperton Hill in the same furrow that the witches' snowball had made. "Wheeeeeeeeeee!" squealed Buster and Polly, not quite sure whether it was brilliant or terrifying or both. Faster and faster and faster they went, rushing through canyons of snow between the shrouded cars. At the bottom of the hill Buster stuck out his foot and steered them past the bus station and out on to the main road. He thought he glimpsed thistledown figures dancing on top of the traffic lights as he shot past, but a spray of powdery snow blinded him for a moment and when he could see again they had vanished.

The road dipped downhill towards the canal, not as steep as the witches' hill but steep enough to keep the old gate moving. It swished through the pedestrian precinct, slaloming between icy statues of shoppers. It flashed past an ornamental fountain where the water had frozen in splattery plumes like modern art. It hit the flat quay beside

the canal, but its speed sent it zooming on, through a field of giant, frozen, red and yellow flowers that turned out to be the umbrellas outside *Luigi's Café*. At the end of the quay, where the path turned sharp right to reach the foot-bridge, the ramshackle sledge kept going. It flew off the canal bank and crashed down on to the frozen canal, where it skated on and on until it hit an old shopping trolley embedded in the ice and slowed, turning in lazy circles and finally coming to a stop.

Buster and Polly were laughing and whooping and gasping for breath, and the silence and the stopping were a shock. They felt suddenly sad. They had come halfway across Smogley in the space of a few minutes, and they both knew that even if they beat the Winter King and lived to be a hundred and two there would never be another sledge-ride like that one, ever. But at least they knew where they were. "The park's only a few streets from here," said Polly. "We can cut back through it to school. . ."

Just then, a little way up-stream, the ice heaved and cracked and a glossy black hump showed under it.

"Dinosaur!" gasped Buster, shoving Polly off the old gate. "Quick!"

He grabbed the wizard's staff and they scrambled and slithered and wobbled across the ice to a stone stairway which led up on to the quay. They looked back just in time to see the ice under their sledge buckle and burst upward. A dark sea-serpent head rose on a long, long neck, huge jaws crunched shut on the splintering wood, slitty nostrils parted to let out a hot snort of breath. For a moment the pale eyes of the water-monster flickered towards Buster, then it gave a huge burp and sank out of sight. The dark water sloshed against the ice, then silence settled over the canal again.

"Crikey!" said Polly. "Your tree-girl was right. All sorts of things have woken up. I've never seen one of *those* in Smogley before. . ."

11
THE FREEZER CENTRE

The park looked more like the North Pole. "We're in the Parktic Circle!" Buster shouted, hurrying through the snow. He was still trembly from the sledge-ride, and excited at the thought of his new-found magical powers. Now he thought about it, perhaps the wizard's staff *had* sort of quivered a bit when he said the magic words. Fancy being a wizard all these years and never knowing!

Polly watched him with a secret smile.

They passed the playground, and the park-keeper's hut where Mr Curd sat entombed in ice with his teacup halfway to his lips. There were strange tracks on the snowy lawns: the great three-toed footprints of trolls and the spidery scribbling of passing icelings. There were no fairy footprints, but as they neared the north gate they heard laughter in the trees and thin voices called down, "Silly humans! Ready for the Big Fight? Oi! Buster, your mum's a *real* lollipop lady now! Come on! Hurry up! The Winter King's waiting!"

"Idiots!" sniffed Buster. "I wish they'd seen me magic you back to life in that garden. Then they'd have a bit more respect. I think I'm going to be pretty good at this wizarding lark. I'll be able to do my homework by magic in future, and next time Masher Harris tries to nick my dinner money I'll turn him into a frog. . ."

For the first time, Polly started to get an uneasy feeling that she might have boosted Buster's self-confidence just a little bit *too* much.

"I'll show this old Winter King a thing or two," he said, twirling his staff like a drum majorette's baton. "I'll have him magicked back inside his hill before you can say 'Harry Potter'."

The closer they drew to Crisp Street, the deeper lay the snow, and they waded and flailed and stumbled through the shoulder-high drifts. As they passed the school the sun came out and gleamed on the icicles that hung from the clock tower and the eaves of the music-room – but all around the town huge banks of cloud were piling up, impossibly dark and fat with snow, getting ready to roll out and spread winter over the rest of the world.

Then they looked out across the playing fields, and gasped as they saw how the Winter King had been passing the time.

Beyond the snowy huddle of TV lorries huge spires of ice were rising above Hob's Hill, sticking themselves together in the same way the icelings had, forming towers and walls and buttresses. The Winter King was building himself a palace from which to rule his ice-bound world. The evening sun glittered coldly on it, and rainbows flew like banners from the topmost turrets. In its cold shadow dozens of icelings stood drawn up in ranks and regiments, covering the playing fields.

Buster tightened his grip on the wizard's staff and ducked behind a snowdrift, pulling Polly down beside him. For a long time they watched the iceling army, but none of the creatures were moving, not one so much as twitched a claw. From time to time they glimpsed the robed figure of the king himself as he strode around at the foot of his amazing ice-castle, gesturing with his staff to add a buttress here, a pinnacle there.

"He's very powerful!" whispered Polly.

"Oh, I could do that, easy," said Buster, but he was secretly starting to wonder if his wizarding skills were really up to taking on the Winter King. Maybe he had let himself get a bit carried away, and just a little bit big-headed. . .

"Let's wait for another day," he said, wriggling down the snowdrift and starting to creep in a homewards direction.

"Buster!" Polly pulled him back. "You're forgetting! There isn't going to be another day! Once the moon comes up, that's it."

"Oh, right. . ."

"You can do it," she assured him.

"OK," said Buster, but as he crept out of the shelter of the snow-bank and started across the playing fields he couldn't shake the feeling that this was going to be the most one-sided contest since Smogley United were drawn to play Liverpool in the FA cup.* But Polly was walking beside him, and the icelings didn't so much as stir as they went by, and by the time he neared the icy entrance of the Winter King's new home he was starting to feel a little bit better.

Oddly enough, the snow around the palace gates was no deeper than it had been yesterday afternoon; a few centimetres of crisp whiteness covering the frozen mud of the football pitches.

*Final score: Smogley nil, Liverpool 17,437.

Buster and Polly crunched quickly across it and up icy stairs into the blue vaults of the palace. Above their heads new spires and staircases were appearing with icy creakings and chimings. In one of the taller spines a TV helicopter hung trapped like a dragonfly in amber.

At the heart of the palace, the outline of Hob's Hill showed dimly through the dark ice of the tower's foundations. Buster thought he could just make out the shapes of his mum and Ian and the others, standing where they had frozen.

In front of them stood a glittering figure, directing the construction work with gestures of its icicle-staff.

Buster's legs wanted to turn and run, his feet wanted to cling fast to the ground, his teeth felt like having a good old chatter and his tummy wouldn't have minded a quick visit to the little boy's room, but his brain told them all not to be stupid and reminded them how easy it had been to de-statuize Polly. They didn't seem particularly convinced, but he managed to lift the staff up in one shivery hand and walk towards the king.

"Oh, be careful!" squeaked Polly.

The Winter King turned. His white face had twisted itself into a new shape, barely recognizable now as Quentin Quigley, and his tinkling robes of ice shone with rainbow light as he came gliding towards Buster.

"What do *you* want?" he said.

Buster's feet ganged up with his legs to have another go at running away, but he managed to control them. "I want my mum back," he said. He tried to sound stern and commanding, but his voice came out as a high-pitched chirrup, like a cartoon mouse. "I want my mum. . ."

"Ah, bless!" sneered the Winter King.

"And I want you to unfreeze everybody else, too," Buster peeped, "and put everything back like it was before and get back in your bottle where the wizards put you."

"In here, you mean?" asked the Winter King. He reached through the ice of his robes and pulled out something that had been frozen there. It was the metal urn that Quentin Quigley had lifted from Hob's Hill, and Buster could see now that its sides were traced with ancient, spidery lettering. Then the Winter King held it close to his face and breathed on it. Hoar frost bloomed on the dark metal and it shattered like a bomb, scattering black fragments over the snowy floor.

"Whoops," the Winter King said, drifting closer.

"Erm, I command you to stop!" Buster ordered,

hoping to sound like one of the sorcerers from the Quirke Brothers' computer games. "Come no further, foul whotsit, or I shall smite thee with, er, with some smites."

The Winter King laughed. "You have no power over me. There is no magic in you. The guardian sleeps; his power is broken. I am free now, and no one can stand against me. Least of all a mere *boy*."

He reached out with his staff, but Polly pulled Buster quickly backwards. "I don't think this was such a good idea!" she said. There was a side-passage in the ice-wall nearby and they darted down it, the Winter King gliding after them.

"I thought you said I could do it!" Buster whimpered. "I thought you said I was magic!"

"Sorry," admitted Polly. "I just thought it might help. . ."

"But I got you de-lawn-ornament-ificated, didn't I?"

"Well, I sort of pretended. . ."

"You what? *Now* you tell me!"

They ran out through a side entrance into the cold of the playing field and the thin sunlight, and heard howls and hoots of mocking laughter. The fairies had gathered on the roofs of the snow-bound *Dig This!* trucks like spectators at a school sports day. "COME ON, BUSTER!" they shouted. "DUFF HIM UP!" They clapped their hands and chanted, "WHO'S GOT A NUMB MUM? BUS-TER!"

And the Winter King came sweeping out of his palace, so close that Buster could feel his numbing breath.

"I'm sorry!" whimpered Polly.

Buster decided to have a last go, for Mum's sake. "Er. . . Stop! Or else!"

"Why should I stop?" hissed the Winter King. "The world is mine; white and quiet and beautiful again, just as it ought to be."

"I'm a wizard," squeaked Buster, holding up the staff.

"No, you're not," sneered the Winter King.

On the TV trucks a fairy shouted, "GIVE ME A 'B'!"

"B!" the rest roared happily.

"GIVE ME A 'U'!"

"U!"

"I'm a bit of a wizard," said Buster, taking a couple of steps backwards as the Winter King advanced.

"GIVE ME AN 'S'!"

"S!"

The Winter King shook his head and smiled. "Pathetic!"

"GIVE ME A 'T'!"

"T!" chanted the fairies.

"Len said the old magic would come to me if I called it, because you froze Mum. . ."

"Oh, yeah?" laughed the Winter King.

"GIVE ME AN 'E'!"

"E!"

"GIVE ME AN 'R'!"

"R!"

"AND WHAT HAVE YOU GOT?"

"Erm . . . UBSRET!!!" hollered the fairies, who couldn't spell.

The Winter King made a lazy little gesture with one finger and Buster felt the wizard's staff go cold, whitening with frost. He snatched his fingers away and it dropped into the snow and sank, and he was all alone and defenceless in front of the Winter King. He looked round for Polly, but she was gone too. She must have panicked and run, he thought, and he couldn't really blame her; she probably wanted to get back home in time for the world's end.

"You're RUBBISH and you KNOW it!" jeered the fairies. "What a nana! Freeze him, Your Majesty!"

But the Winter King had no more interest in Buster: he wanted to go back to work on his beautiful palace. He clicked his fingers and said, "Deal with him," and one of the waiting icelings sprang to life and came spidering towards Buster, lifting its claws. It was the one with the crisp-packet frozen into its face, and at the sight of it Buster's body suddenly got the better of his brain and started to run, slipping and scrabbling over the snow with the creature close behind. When he reached the TV trucks he turned and pulled the catapult from his pocket and fired his heaviest stone at it, but the iceling was thicker than when he had fought with it yesterday, and the stone just bounced off, leaving a white star like a medal on its chest. The watching fairies jeered and danced and pelted Buster with snowballs. "YOU'RE GONNA GET YOUR HEAD KICKED IN!" they chanted.

The iceling inched forward, and Buster tried to stand there and wait for its touch so that the fairies on the truck would see how brave he was and stop their hoots and cat-calls. But he couldn't even manage that. As the icy claws reached out for him he took a helpless step back, and then another and another, and suddenly a round, bespectacled shape darted out from behind the nearest of the TV trucks and shouted, "Stop that this instant!"

The iceling turned.

Polly came pounding across the snow towards it, waving around her head something black and yellow and vaguely familiar. It was Mum's lollipop sign, and it hit the iceling in its middle and shattered it into roughly 10,000,000 pieces.

"Nice one, Polly!" squeaked Buster.

"OOOOOOH!" chorused the fairies. "That's CHEATING!"

"Metal," said Polly, holding out the lollipop. "I don't think the Winter King likes metal. That's why the urn they'd stuck him in was made of iron. And metal is supposed to protect against enchantments; I read it in your Mum's folklore book. . ."

The Winter King heard the sharp *kisssh* of the breaking ice and spun about, rushing down on Buster, while his army of icelings sprang into jerky life behind him. Backed up against the TV truck, Buster and Polly had nowhere to run to, but as the Winter King stretched out his staff Buster swung the lollipop and smashed it in two.

The Winter King looked amazed. "Oooh! You cheeky little –"

There hadn't been any metal around when the Winter King first stalked the world . . . or at least, it had all been tidily tucked away inside mountains. Metal unnerved him. Cars and lorries and corrugated tin roofs and the zips on people's trousers had not been too much of a problem – he had just frozen them along with everything else. But being attacked by this terrible metal staff with its round, painted metal flag at the top was a different matter. He'd been hoping that, with all the wizards gone, nobody would remember his weakness. Now, these two interfering kids had worked it out! He took a frightened step backwards, and Buster made another great scything swing with the lollipop, and this time it hit the Winter King's head.

There was a bang so loud that it sounded to Buster as if the world had snapped in two. It was so loud that it cracked the icelings into pieces and brought the Winter King's palace crashing down in shards and splinters and shook icicles off roofs all across Smogley. It was so loud that, in the cavern under *The Nine Dancers*, the sleeping wizard opened his eyes and sat up straight to ask, "Eh? What was that? What's happening? Where's me staff?"

Quentin Quigley's dazed body flopped over into the snow and a pale fog lifted from him, man-shaped at first, but quickly blurring and spreading.

Buster looked at Polly. Had they won? She shrugged. Even the fairies weren't sure, and had fallen quiet for once. He studied the snow, expecting it to melt, but it didn't. The fog that had spilled out of Quentin Quigley twisted itself into strange, frightening shapes. Two pale gleams of light hung near the heart of it, colder than cold. It was the Winter King.

It swirled over Quentin Quigley's body, trying to find a way back in, but the TV presenter's mind wasn't up to much at the best of times and after its adventures with the Winter King and that whack with the lollipop it was taking a well-earned rest. The fog reached away towards Hob's Hill and wrapped itself around Mum, then Ian, then one of the other archaeologists, but their bodies were running too slow inside their mummy-cases of ice to be of any use yet to the Winter King, and he was too angry to wait for them to thaw. But there was another body nearby that he could use, and he billowed towards it.

"Argh!" shouted Buster as the fog rushed down on him. He swiped at it with the lollipop and Polly swung punches, but there was nothing to hit, and the fog closed around him, chill and blinding white. He dropped the lollipop. He could feel the Winter King groping for a handhold in his brain and he tried to think of warm things; sizzling hot dogs and suntan lotion and the prickly feel of salt drying on your back on a warm beach. But the thoughts all turned cold: frozen chipolatas, suntan-lotion lollies and the tingle of frostbite on the shores of an ice-bound sea. And then the fog was inside him and he could see clearly again, and he realized for the first time how beautiful Smogley looked under its wrapping of snow, and how pure and pale was the sunlight on the deep drifts, and how wonderfully quiet it all was and how clean the air. *I shouldn't have fought the Winter King*, he thought. *I've been on the wrong side! He was right all along, it's much better like this. . .*

Then a great shuddering *bong* broke his train of thought, and he went reeling back against the side of the TV truck and realized that Polly had just walloped him round the back of the head with Mum's lollipop. "Ouch!" he said. "That really hurt!"

"Sorry," said Polly. "It was for your own good. . . Should I do it again, just to be on the safe side?"

"No way!" Buster shook the creeping coldness from his head and looked around. The fog hung in the sky above his head, a furious egg of white vapour that spun end-over-end and spat out cold sparks, buzzing like a power-line on a frosty morning. Mixed in with the buzzing was another noise, a noise that hadn't been heard in Smogley for a night and a day – the roar of an engine. A smell of petrol came eddying across the playing field, startling after the hard white smell of the snow, and Buster looked round and saw a motorbike speeding towards him, the wizard from the cavern crouching low over the handlebars.

"He's awake!" shouted Buster.

The speeding wizard slammed on his brakes and shot over the handlebars, landing on his bottom next to Polly. He stood up, tugging off his crash-helmet and unwrapping his beard, which he had wound round his neck like a long scarf. "A strange steed," he muttered, peering at the fallen bike. "Enchanted, no doubt. It appears to be a cross between a dragon and a wheelbarrow." He rubbed his hands and cracked his knuckles. Above him the fog that was the Winter King hissed and fizzed and reached out fierce tentacles of mist, but they jerked back as if stung when they touched the wizard's long, grey robes.

"Now then," said the wizard, glancing at Buster, "let's get to work. It's a good thing for you, boy, that I turned up when I did."

Buster was speechless with indignation. He wanted to say, "*Well, if I hadn't come here and challenged him, and Polly hadn't walloped the iceling with that lollipop, you'd never even have woken up!*" – but there was something a bit headmastery about the old man that warned him not to try and argue.

"Staff!" said the wizard, and it leaped out of the snow and into his hand, crackling with orange flames.

"Vessel!" he ordered. Nothing happened. He snapped his fingers and said, "Vessel!" again, then turned to Buster. "Where is it, boy?"

"You mean that old metal urn thing?" Buster looked sheepishly down at his feet and drew a circle in the snow with the toe of one trainer. "It's broken."

"Broken?" The wizard's bushy eyebrows twisted into an angry frown. "Broken? But how am I to bind the Winter King without a Vessel of Power to bind him *in*?"

"Well, it wasn't Buster's fault," said Polly.

Overhead the Winter King made spitty laughing noises. He had grown larger and colder and his tentacles of fog did not draw back quite so quickly now when they touched the wizard's robes.

"I'll find you something else!" Buster promised. He took off his rucksack and started hunting desperately through the stuff inside

"Something else?" said the wizard sarcastically, dodging a crackle of icy lightning from the Winter King. "You cannot bind the Winter King in any common vessel, boy! Do you think I can lock him up in a cup or a pudding-bowl? It must be something dwarf-wrought and woven with words of power. . . Ooh! What's this?" He looked down in surprise at the thermos flask Buster had thrust at him. "It is metal – but like no metal I have ever seen before. . . Strong magic for sure. And these figures drawn upon it. . . They are the gods of your tribe, no doubt?"

"They're just some TV characters," said Buster humbly. "That one's called Po, and that one's Tinky-Winky. . ."

Another bolt of icy fire flashed past, shearing fifteen centimetres off the bottom of the wizard's beard. The Winter King was as tall as the sky, a tower of coldness looming over the playing fields. Quickly, the wizard opened the flask and shook out the dregs of the hot chocolate. Then he held it up towards the fog.

"I command you to sleep!" he shouted. "In the name of the Brotherhood of Wizards I bind you in

this . . . er . . . Flask of Power, and hold you there with the three great spells that have been handed down from wizard to wizard since the world was young: Abracadabra! Nicky-Nacky-Noo! Shazam!"

Buster wasn't sure he had heard right, but there was no time to ask for a repeat of the magic words. The white fog was starting to spin like a blob of cream in a well-stirred mug of coffee, and as it spun it spiralled downward, crackling with helpless rage, until the last of it had vanished into the thermos flask. The wizard clapped the lid on and twisted it tight. The faintest buzzing came from inside, the faintest touch of hoar frost blanched the plastic, then it was over. The wizard stowed the flask inside his robes. "I'll take care of this," he announced, like a teacher confiscating someone's spud-gun.

"Will you put him back in Hob's Hill?" asked Buster.

"Don't be silly, boy!" The wizard scowled at him. "The way you mortals keep meddling, he'd be out again in another six months. No, I shall build a new barrow for him to rest in, somewhere far away where he'll be undisturbed until it's the right time for another ice age. There is no room for magic around *here* any more."

"So what about the trolls and the icelings?" asked Buster.

"Oh, that's all over," said the wizard, climbing aboard his motorbike. "They'll not trouble you any more." He revved the engines. "Oooh, I like this!"

"And the fairies?" said Polly. On top of the TV trucks the fairies were still cavorting, twisting the aerials into rude words and building snowmen.

"Oh, yes. . ." muttered the wizard, without much interest. He flipped his staff at them and a whirlwind sprang up and drifted to and fro across the lorries, hoovering up the fairies. When they were all trapped inside it he said, "Outer Mongolia, I think," and snapped his fingers.

"Argh! Booo! Unfair to fairies!" wailed the fairies, a giddy blur vanishing in the general direction of the Gobi Desert.

"Good day, children," said the wizard, stuffing his staff into a saddlebag. "Don't go mucking about with magic any more. You're really not cut out for it, you know."

"But what about Mum and everybody? They're still frozen! You can't leave them like this!"

"We'll just have to let nature take its course," replied the wizard. "I only really do bindings and banishings, you see. Unfreezing people really isn't my department." And with that he gunned the engine and the bike went bellowing off across the snow-fields and away up Dancers Road, the sound of its engine growing fainter and fainter until it faded into the silence.

Buster and Polly stood and looked at each other. They had both thought that once the Winter King had been defeated everything would return to normal, but the snow was still all around them and Mrs Bayliss and the others were still frozen statues on Hob's Hill.

"Oh!" moaned Buster in despair.

"Ow!" groaned a voice near his feet, sounding like a not-very-good echo.

Quentin Quigley was sitting up and opening his eyes, which had returned to their normal colour. "Ow, my *head*!" he muttered. "Oh, hi kid. . . Is it just me, or has it suddenly got a bit chilly?" Then he looked down and saw his bare pink body in its *Dig This!* boxer-shorts, drenched with ice-water from the melted robes. "Argh! What's happening!" he yelled. "Where did my clothes go! They're designer labels, you know! What have you rotten kids done with them?"

But Buster wasn't listening. He was charging off across the football pitch towards Hob's Hill, where the frozen figures were slowly coming to life, shaking themselves free of the thin clear ice that fell away from them in shards and vanished into nothingness before it hit the ground. The huge fragments of the Winter King's castle faded like mist, freeing trapped birds which flapped away with puzzled cheeps and releasing the pilots of the helicopter, who stumbled from the wreckage of their machine and scratched their heads. Up at the top of the hill Buster's mum was saying, "Oh! Where did all that *snow* come from?" and Ian was asking her, "Did you feel something just then? A sort of shivery feeling, like someone walking over your grave. . ."

Before she could answer, Buster cannoned into her and almost knocked her off her feet. "Steady!" she laughed. "What on earth's the matter? And why are you all wrapped up like that? You must be sweltering!" And Buster realized that he *was* a bit hot inside his scarf and his parka and his sweatshirt and his spare jumper, under the blazing summer sun.

12
THAWING OUT

"And finally," said the newsreader on the TV that night, "it's been 'snow' laughing matter in Smogley today, where freak blizzards cut the town off from the outside world for almost twenty-four hours! Oddly enough, nobody in Smogley remembers seeing the snow fall. One of Britain's top brain specialists said today, "The people of Smogley seem to be suffering from a harmless loss of memory. It might have been caused by the sudden drop in temperature, but we're not really sure; I suppose it's just one of those things." She beamed across the studio at weatherman Michael Fishcake and said, "So, Michael, what do you think of that?"

"Well, Trixie," he chuckled, "you've got to hand it to the great British weather, haven't you? It's full *of surprises! Do you like my new jumper, by the way? Look, it's got clouds and rainbows and things on it. . ."*

Buster and Polly both sighed, sitting together beside Buster's mum on the squelchy sofa in his soggy living room. They had just been through the most exciting, scary, dangerous twenty-four hours of their lives and all the grown-ups could talk about was the *weather*! But they both knew there was no point trying to explain what had really happened. Even the Quirke Brothers hadn't believed it when Buster tried to tell them about the icelings and the Winter King. Only he and Polly knew the truth.

Still, at least nobody seemed any the worse for having been frozen. The only side-effect was that they all kept thinking about cold things the whole time. All over Smogley people were buying ice creams and fridges and freezers and fans, and the queues outside the ice-rink stretched three times round the block, but Buster expected it would pass.

Mum squelched across the carpet to switch the TV off. As the ice thawed, the whole house had been turned into a giant cold shower by water pouring down from burst pipes in the loft. Looking at the damage, Mum said, "This is going to cost a fortune to repair. It's such a pity. I really fancied a holiday this year. I was thinking we could go to Norway or Iceland or Alaska... Somewhere with icebergs." She shook her head sadly. "Oh, well, I think there's still half an arctic roll in the freezer. Shall we have some?"

"Mummy and Daddy are just the same," whispered Polly, who had popped home earlier to check that her parents were behaving themselves without her. "They've just booked a weekend break in northern Siberia. It sounds horrible. Do you think your mum would let me stay here instead?"

They splished after Buster's mum into the kitchen. Evening sunlight spilled in through the open windows and they could hear the familiar snore and grumble of traffic. Shrill shouts of laughter echoed over the rooftops, but it was only the neighbourhood children running down to the park with their sledges before the last snow melted. In the middle of the garden the ash tree stood looking forlorn, with meltwater dripping off its frost-burnt leaves.

"Mum?" asked Buster. "Can we do something with that tree?"

"Like a swing?" she said. "Or a tree-house?"

"NO!" he cried, so loudly that she almost

dropped the arctic roll. "No, I just think it needs looking after. Some better soil and compost and manure and things like that."

Mum looked at him as if she thought he was joking. "This is all very sudden. You've never been interested in gardening before. But yes, if you like. . ."

The doorbell rang. At least, it would have rung if it hadn't been full of water. As it was, it managed to make a feeble little noise like a drowning gerbil going under for the third time. Buster ran to the door and opened it to find Ian and Carla standing on the front step. "We brought some ice cream," they said, coming in.

Mum spread some bin-liners over the wet chairs so that everybody could sit down.

"We're here because Quentin Quigley has gone a bit odd," said Carla, looking awkward, "I mean, even odder than before."

"He says he's going to give up presenting *Dig This!*" explained Ian. "He's suddenly decided he wants to open up a worldwide chain of ice cream restaurants called 'Winter Kings'. I can't think what's got into him."

"So we need a new presenter," said Carla, "and Ian suggested. . ."

"I thought you might like to do it, Erica," said

the archaeologist nervously. "I mean, you're keen and you know a lot more about history than Quentin Quigley ever did, and you're used to working with children."

"Well, I don't know," said Buster's mum, in that way grown-ups have of saying 'I don't know' when in fact they know perfectly well and are so excited that their socks are about to explode. "What do you think, Buster?"

"I think it would be great!" said Buster. "You could get these blokes on dressed up as knights and pirates and Vikings and stuff and make them have a big fight! And I've got all kinds of other ideas you could put in. . ."

"Well, I'm still not sure I could. . ." said Mum, modestly.

"Of course she'll do it!" shouted Polly.

"That's settled then," grinned Carla, before Mum could say any more. "*Dig This!* with Erica Bayliss! Of course, the Hob's Hill programme will have to be cancelled – I can't remember if we found anything or not, but all this snow has played such havoc with the schedules that I think we'd better start from scratch with the next dig. . ."

Buster and Polly left them talking and went out into the garden with their bowls of ice cream. They sat down beside the ash tree and listened to

Mum's happy laughter drifting from the open door.

The ice cream was lemon meringue flavour, Buster's favourite, but instead of finishing it he made sure nobody was watching him and put the last scoop down between the tree's mossy roots. "There you go," he said.

The ash tree rustled its branches at him, although there was hardly any wind.

"I'm sorry I fibbed to you," said Polly. "I mean, making you think you had magical powers and everything. It must have been a bit disappointing to find out you were just ordinary after all."

"Oh, that's all right," said Buster. "I mean, it would have been fun, being able to do magic and stuff. But I'd probably have had to keep running around fighting the forces of evil and everything, and it is the school holidays. I've got better things to do. . ."

THE END